Neandergirl

John Himmelman

Neandergirl

Pegasus

PEGASUS PAPERBACK

© Copyright 2023
John Himmelman

A CIP catalogue record for this title is available from the British Library

ISBN-978-1-91090-379-7

*Pegasus is an imprint of
Pegasus Elliot MacKenzie Publishers Ltd.*
www.pegasuspublishers.com

First Published in 2023

**Pegasus
Sheraton House Castle Park
Cambridge CB3 0AX England**

Printed & Bound in Great Britain

For my beloved family,
past, present, and future

Foreword

Neanderthals (*Homo neanderthalensis*) were an ancient species of human who migrated from Africa and into Europe and Asia over 400,000 years ago. They mysteriously disappeared about 40,000 years ago, right around the arrival of our species, *Homo sapiens*. The two species did mingle, and many of us carry within our genes a smidgeon of Neanderthal DNA.

The Neanderthals were a powerfully built species, with keen eyesight and hearing. Their people hunted great mammoths, elk, and bison face-to-face. They were in turn hunted by cave bears, wolves, saber-toothed cats, and other large predators.

The Neanderthals were also intelligent. They lived together in small groups, made stone and bone tools, and carried out various rituals. There is little evidence, however, they were driven to create art, as we their relatives did, and do. Could they have?

It is highly reasonable to believe that some shone in ways others did not.

Chapter 1

Jennifer Moore walked along the base of the desert ridge. Her eyes watered in the sun's glare, bending the landscape as she searched the surroundings. They fell upon a small bump in the steep outcropping ahead. It was so small; it would have escaped anyone else's notice. Sometimes, but rarely, such bumps turned out to be a partially exposed fossil. Chances were far better it was just a rock, but she had a feeling for these things that went beyond the terrain itself. It came from years of hunting for breaks in the patterns, desert features that seemed slightly out of place. This one almost screamed for her attention. It called to her. She climbed hand over foot up the hill to where it leveled off and bent down for a closer look.

"Hm-hm-hmm." She pulled a brush from her bag and swept away some of the loose gravel. The archeologist drew back and gasped. She was looking at a fully intact face on a skull! The back of its head lay buried just up to the cheekbones. It brought to mind the image of a swimmer doing the backstroke through the sand.

Her colleague, and boss, Dr Stanley Hirnhoff, was off in the distance. Drew and Jordan, the two student interns, were with him. Jen looked back down at the fossil. She dropped to her knees and began to pick and scrape away at the soft, encasing stone. She had half the skull free when she glanced over and saw a hand.

"An intact skeleton?" she asked herself, trying to contain her excitement. That would be hoping for too much. She moved off the skull and to the hand. Its fingers were wrapped around a short, rod-shaped object.

"What is *this* now? Broken spear?"

Jen ran her fingers across its surface. The object came easily free, and she picked it up. A breeze stirred the stillness. It blew through her, and she shivered in the 110-degree heat. A clear vision of her mother entered her mind. *Mom? Why are you in my head now?* She looked at the rod. *No, not spear. Animal bone. Bird?* Then she noticed a series of holes along the side.

"Drilled holes! *Flute*!" she said aloud. She looked up to find Hirnhoff. He and the interns were still shouting distance away.

Without thinking, she stuffed the flute in her pocket. *Wait! Why am I doing this? No!* She reached back in her pocket to put in back it in place, but something unseen stopped her. Unseen, but with unyielding strength. She could not make herself remove it. *I have to keep this! I don't know why but I... just have to! This is crazy!*

Jen stood up. "Dr Hirnhoff, over here!" she shouted, her voice shaky. *What if he finds out what I did?* "Hurry! Hurry!"

"I doubt anything you found is going anywhere, Jen," the archeologist shouted back.

"Bones! Human, but might not be, exactly," she said.

The doctor stopped what he was doing, and he and the interns rushed to join her.

"You of all people should know the difference between *Homo sapiens* and other animals," said the professor, fighting for breath in the heat as he crawled up the ridge.

"I do, Stan. What I meant was it's a hominid, but I think not our species. Neanderthal, maybe?"

Dr Hirnhoff rushed over to where his colleague was digging. He looked at the partially exposed skull.

"Oh my," he said. "That brow… Yes! I think you could be correct! Keep going, Jen."

Drew peered over the shoulders of the other two. This was his first dig, and his interest was mostly in prehistoric plants. "How can you tell which is which?" he asked.

"There are differences," said Jen.

"And we're related to these, right?" he asked.

"*Homo neanderthalensis* — Neanderthals — and *us—Homo sapiens* — lived side by side for a few thousand years," said Dr Hirnhoff. "And there was some gene mixing going on. Many of us today carry

Neanderthal DNA. But they were not our species. They're older than us and grew on a different branch of the evolutionary tree."

"Like apes," said Jordan.

"Not exactly," said Hirnhoff. "*Neanderthalensis* were more… intelligent. If things had gone differently, they could have been here digging *us* up. They ran the show here for over four hundred thousand years."

Jen cleared away more of the skull. "And then they disappeared," she said. "Stan, this is a Neanderthal. There's no question. You two, look at how heavy the brow is over the eye sockets. The wide nasal passage…"

"She's right. Clear away more around the cheek," said her colleague. "There it is! Look at those beautiful high cheekbones!"

"We have a Neanderthal!" said Jen.

"I believe we do!" agreed Stan.

"And," began Jen. She took away some more of the sand. "It seems to be a young one. An older child?"

"I think so, Jen. Good teeth, not very worn yet, but fully developed. Teen, maybe?"

"Maybe—Jordan, watch your feet! There's a hand right there."

The intern jumped. "Whoa, sorry! Is it still connected to the body?"

"Don't know," said Jen. "We need to clear this out some more. The substrate and surface material's pretty soft for the first foot or so. I think we can pull most of it free right here. We wrap it, box it, and bring it home. You agree, Stan?”

“Yes. A full skeleton would be amazing. A lot to wish for, but it happens. This had to have been exposed fairly recently, I’d say within the last couple years. Likely from a good rain. Explains what good shape it’s in.” He dragged his walking stick in a large oval around the skull and where the body might be. “Jordan, Drew, set up the tarp to get us out of this sun. We’ll sift through the soft upper layers of sand and then start chipping away inside this circle. Careful, though, everyone!”

“I know, scorpions,” said Jordan.

“Yes, that, too. But be careful you don’t chip into a bone. They could be scattered. We want all the pieces. And we don’t know how many that will be yet. They could be scattered for who knows how far.”

“Is it a he or a she?” asked Drew.

“Hard to tell right now,” said Dr Hirnhoff.

“She,” said Jen.

Hirnhoff laughed. “And you know this how?”

Jen stood and looked down at the skull. Its stone-packed eye sockets looked back up at her. She absently grasped the flute in her pocket. *Looking forward to meeting you,* she said silently to the ancient young Neanderthal.

“I just know,” she answered. “Not science. Just me knowing. Funny, huh.”

Chapter 2

Skeetu was stalking frogs in the marsh when she heard Bulo wailing in the distance. Uncle's son had never screamed like that before and the sound of it shook her body with the chill of fear. She raced back to their cave and stopped at the entrance. Inside, Mother, Father, and Uncle were dead. A cave bear, its massive body nearly filling the room, hunched over Bulo, who was bleeding badly from his side. The claws of the beast had ripped through the tough woolly rhino hide that hung from his shoulders.

"*Run!*" he cried, but Skeetu picked up Father's spear and thrust it at the bear. The sharp stone tip broke off in its thigh and it turned and snarled at the girl. She nearly froze, seeing the blood on its mouth, the blood of her family. Bulo got to his feet and pounded on the bear with his stone ax, drawing it away from her. With a swipe of its arm, the enraged animal sent the boy flying into the wall. He crumpled to the floor.

"*Bulo!*" The girl lunged at the cave bear with the shaft of her spear and missed. It lurched forward, but she darted just out of reach. She ran outside of the cave and climbed a tree. She knew this was a mistake and that it would climb up after her, but she had no time to think of anything better. The bear followed. It began to pull itself up the tree, its claws shredding the bark in long strips. Skeetu could feel the beast's hot breath on her leg as it snapped at her foot. Its teeth clacked loudly, like the clapping of river stones.

"*Down here!*" shouted a voice from below. Bulo had left the cave and stabbed his spear into the bear. The bear dropped to the ground, injured, but not dead. With a surprising burst of speed, it leapt at the boy. He fell to the ground and then scrambled to his feet and ran back into to cave.

"*Not there!*" screamed Skeetu! "Don't go back *in* there!" She could do nothing but watch the beast follow after him. There followed a horrid, sickening sound, one that would never leave her memory, and the bear limped out of the entrance. It looked up at the girl in the tree, as if deciding if she was worth the effort to chase.

"*Go! Go!*" shouted Skeetu, waving her arms. The bear lingered a moment longer and then shook its hide and lumbered off.

Skeetu climbed down and walked to the mouth of the cave. She knew what she would see and did not want to go in there. But she knew she had to.

What the young Neanderthal did *not* know, nor would ever, was that the four killed by that cave bear were among the very last of her kind. In her seasons on the land, she had never seen another of the *old kind*, or *oldkin* as Mother called them. *Her* kind. The new kind, *sahaar,* now walked among them. And her family had done all they could to avoid them. Uncle said they came from across the great lakes on the backs of turtles. And that they could become trees at night. He said his father had seen a whole forest of them. Once Uncle saw one across the river and it called out to him. "Sahaar! Sahaar!" it said.

"I think it was trying to tell me what it is," said Uncle.

"Or telling you what it thought you were," said Father.

***

Two summers and a winter had passed since Skeetu lost her family to the cave bear. She had learned to live on her own. She caught fish in the lake and ate the shellfish along the shore. Land creatures, prey with fur, feathers, and scales were hunted with her spear. She wasn't as good at it as others in her clan had been, but she got better. Her small size made her little match for the larger aurochs and caribou. Hares were easier. Groundpigs easier yet. The girl had learned from Uncle what plants to eat. Some were pulled from the ground; some from water, to get to the roots. Others offered tasty seeds or bore juicy berries.

The air was still this morning. The warm season was drawing to an end. Skeetu would miss it, as she always did. She sat frozen in place behind a tree and listened for the bird.

"Seweeet… seweeet…" came the call from the edge of the meadow.

The oldkin pushed the tip of her tongue lightly against the roof of her mouth and whistled, imitating the sound, "Seweeet… seweeet."

The bird answered. She answered back. Another bird popped up on the shrub behind her and joined them in song.

Skeetu smiled, ending the chorus. Smiling made whistling difficult. It didn't matter. The song was now her own. It would be added to the others and brought out whenever she wished to hear it.

The girl left the marsh to head to the great lake. She was hungry. There would be shellfish buried where the tide met the rocky shore. She whistled her new tune along the way. It made her think of Father, who always thought it a waste of time, singing like birds.

"How will those sounds you make, feed us? How will they keep us warm?" he'd ask.

"She could call them in closer," said Uncle. "Then we catch them!" He made a comical grabbing motion with his hands.

"They are too small to eat," said Skeetu.

"See?" grunted Father. "A waste."

The girl walked along the shore, searching for longclams. She sang a new tune to herself, adding the sounds she'd learned earlier. She had been the only one in her family who could do this, and she wasn't sure where it came from. The birds helped teach her, she knew. They made sounds to please her ears. Why shouldn't she do the same? She was more than a bird. She wondered if the birds, her teachers, thought they were more than an oldkin?

Mother had enjoyed listening to her. She said it brought to mind the coming of spring, but when she tried to imitate her daughter, she sounded like a dying caribou. It made Skeetu laugh.

"Do not mock your mother," Mother would say. "Those sounds are not *your* gift, they are mine."

"Do you mean they are *my* gift? Since I can do this and no one else can?"

"No," said Mother. "It is a gift for me as I get to hear it from you."

Skeetu collected a handful of clams and sat on a rock to work the food from the tight shells. She looked down in the sand and saw a footprint. It was fairly fresh. She pressed her foot next to it, to make a print. Hers was much wider, and a little longer.

"Sahaar," she said to herself. The girl stood and looked around. No one was there, at least that she could see.

"Hohoo?" she called. There was no answer.

The girl wrapped the clams in her hare skin pouch and followed the footprints. They led to a grassy plain that belonged to the mammoths. She didn't like to go there, with their deep chested grunts and great sharp tusks. The prints disappeared over the rocks at the base of a hill. Satisfied she was alone, she sat again to work on her meal. She put down the skin and spread out her longclams. As she searched the ground for a thin rock to pry them open, she saw something lying in the dirt. Skeetu crawled to it and picked it up. *Hollow bone. Bear leg? Maybe.* Bones were not a rare find, and often, with some scraping and crushing, they were food. This one was different. It had been hollowed out and carved smooth and had four neat holes drilled in the side. *How would those get there? Worms? Teeth?*

Skeetu put the bone on top of the clams and wrapped them in the skin. With a look over her shoulder to make sure no one was watching; she ran back home to her cave in the valley bottom.

Chapter 3

Jen studied the flute beneath the magnifying light in her kitchen. *Why do I have this? What made me take it?* Stealing an artifact from a dig was wrong for so many reasons! It took away a clue that could be used to piece together a puzzle, and in this case, one guaranteed to be of great groundbreaking significance. It changed the story of *neanderthalensis*. But worse yet, it was stealing from the past. She knew better than most why this should not be done, but she also knew that she had to do it. It was the *why* that haunted her.

She flipped through the pages of her manuals on bird bones found in archaeological sites. *Crane? Grus grus?* It looked like a good fit. But how did such a delicate thing survive 40,000 years, when time and the elements would so easily grind it to dust?

The bones, from a girl believed to be in her early-to-late teens, whom she dubbed *Neandergirl*, were excavated from the site in Spain and brought back to her museum in the United States. They rested in a wooden crate in the basement where, in time, the team would get to examine them fully. As exciting a find as they were, there was a long backlog of bone-filled boxes to sort through before anyone got to these.

Jen would have given this find a higher priority, though. While it turned out not to be a complete skeleton, nearly a quarter of it was largely intact. Missing were the lower torso and the left arm and hand. A few toes were found, for both feet, suggesting that the skeleton came to rest intact but was broken up either by river currents or scavengers.

"How often do we find such a well-preserved Neanderthal?" she'd asked Dr Hirnhoff.

"Us? This is a first," he agreed. "But there are some better than this—not here, unfortunately, but out there in collections. Or still in crates, like ours."

"We unearthed her from a beautiful sunny desert to stick her in a coffin—in a basement," said Jen. She knew the situation, but it was still frustrating.

"You're dark today," said her colleague. "We'll get to it. Believe me, I'd love to spend time with this one. I think it's fairly newer than some of the others that have been found in that region. Could be from their last hurrah on this planet." He gestured to the crowded room, filled with artifacts. "But what about all this? Who will catalogue and analyze the fieldwork that's already been done? We have actual *Homo sapiens* to sort, or pieces of them, anyway. It's basically just you and myself, and some of our graduate students who know just enough to not send us too far backwards."

"I know," said Jen. "Nothing you're telling me is something I don't know."

"We have months of work to get through. Which is good, yes? Means we've been having some luck in the field. Feel free to poke around—in your *spare* time—if you think you can find something ground breaking."

Of course, had she left the flute intact in the girl's hand, Neandergirl would have been pushed to the top of the list. While prehistoric people were known to make musical instruments, it was the modern humans, *Homo sapiens,* who were credited with this ability. She'd long known that Neanderthals were not the weak-minded brutes they were once thought to be. They survived in Ice Age Europe for over 400,000 years before our own human ancestors arrived, which, maybe not coincidentally, was about when they disappeared about 40,000 years ago. They were smart and resourceful. They made tools. They looked after their weak and sick; they buried their dead. They may have made simple marks in stone to communicate, but they were not the renowned artists who left behind the mesmerizing cave paintings in France and other parts of the world. Again, that was *sapiens*—the human beings who became us. And Neanderthals were not known to make musical instruments. *Could they have? Of course*, thought the archeologist. But to date there had not been solid evidence to back it up. *Maybe I found it.*

True, there *was* that possibility. But there were others, as well. *Homo neanderthalensis* existed alongside *Homo sapiens* for 3,000 years, likely longer. People today are walking around with Neanderthal

DNA in their genes, proof we did more than just coexist. *Maybe its original creator lost it*, she thought. *Did she steal it? No! Neandergirl wouldn't do that!* Jen laughed at herself.

"Defending a girl gone since the Stone Age!" she said. *But no*, she thought. *She wouldn't have stolen it. I don't know if stealing even happened then, in the way that we know it. But who knows, maybe stealing is what makes us human. But Neandergirl was a different kind of human, technically...*

Jen turned off the light and closed her books. She whistled for Dugg, her German Shepherd. He was rarely far from her and walked over from the other side of the room.

"This bone is a no-no," she said to the dog, scratching him behind the ear.

Her eyes were burning from staring at the thing for so long—she could no longer focus. She picked up the flute and brought it into bed. It was heavier than it would have been, the riverbed silt having hardened inside it. She knew that filling was what had kept it intact for so long. As always, whenever in her hand, her fingertips danced over the holes, as if playing a silent tune. There was a story it would tell her—a song it would sing. She knew this beyond any doubt. The archeologist stared at it through tired eyes, a blurry gray paleness in the darkened room. *Okay, enough for now...* She gently placed it on the dresser by the bed. Dugg watched her, waiting for the invitation.

"Come on up, boy," said Jen, patting the bed. The dog jumped up and the two drifted off to sleep.

That night, she dreamed about when she was a child.

Chapter 4

Skeetu sat on a smooth log in her cave. The air was brisk, and she fed a small fire by the entrance. She didn't really need it yet, but the heat felt good on her skin, and staring into the flames made her think of things that had once happened, and things she might do on another day. The fire was born of embers collected from a tree struck by lightning two moon passes ago. Keeping them alive was part of her daily work. Once they died, there'd be no more fire until lightning struck another tree, which only happened in the warm season.

The longclams were gone, taking with them her hunger. She held the bear bone in her hands, rolling it in her fingers. She wondered if it was made by the sahaar whose footprint she found.

"Why do they put holes in this?" she asked herself. "For the soft meat inside?" The sahaar did some curious things; at least that's what she was told. The prints at the lake were as close as she'd ever come to one. The girl held the bone up to her eye, to look through it. A pebble stuck inside blocked her view and she tried to shake it out. When that failed to dislodge it, she brought it to her mouth and gave a blow. That pushed it free, but with a curious sound. She blew through the end again, and gasped! It sounded like a bird, but more… *hollow*? She tried tipping the bone at different angles and was able to coax it to produce a long, steady whistle. In doing this, her finger blocked one of the holes in the side, changing the sound.

"Oooo!"

Skeetu spent the evening experimenting with different finger combinations to see how many sounds she could make. She was still playing long after the fire settled into its ember bed.

***

Over the next few months, Skeetu stole every moment she could to make her flute sing. She had spent most of her years imitating birds and had already discovered a love for making sounds to please to her ears. Those sounds came from inside her chest and were set free past her lips. It brought her joy hear them. And sometimes sadness. But that sadness, in an odd way, became a kind of joy in its release. The flute could make sounds that she could not make with her lips alone. There was now nothing she wished to do more. At times she would play so long she'd forget to eat, or sleep. She'd wondered if she could make more of these singing bones and tried many times. It always ended in frustration. Something would always be a little off, or a lot off. And when she did manage to make one that could produce a sound, it was not a sound like from the one she found, and it was not a sound she wished to hear.

***

The long winter had settled in and finding food became more difficult. She hunted along the ice-crusted river for water mice and hares. One hare would feed her for a couple days, along with the shriveled fruit from the shrubs further up the banks. She could always peel back the tough skin of the trees to chew on the softer skin beneath, but that was only if she could not do better. She found the tracks of a fox and followed them. While it would be a hard animal to sneak up on, she had done so before and it would feed her for a little bit longer than a hare. And the bushy fur tail wrapped around her neck would help keep her warm. Skeetu came upon some new footprints. They were larger and similar to her own. They covered the fox tracks, which told her that whatever made those tracks were hunting the fox, too. And it looked as if there were more than one animal making them.

"Sahaar," she whispered, and followed where they led. The tracks were different from what she had seen along the lake a time ago. She looked down at her own feet, wrapped in elk hide. "They cover their feet, too!"

The tracks went over the ice on the river for a few steps, and then returned to the bank. Skeetu stopped. *Foolish to try it at all this time of the season! The ice is too thin.* She had fallen in winter water before. Her body had gone instantly numb. If Uncle had not heard her call for help, she'd be asleep in the mud below. She turned around and climbed up a small hill to have a better look at her surroundings. A pile of rocks sat at the top, gathered by Father a time before Mother brought her to breath in the valley. At that time, there were more in her clan. They had died before she came along, but she'd heard many of their names in stories. There was Banor, killed hunting mammoths, and his brother Bint, also killed hunting mammoths. Skent fell from a tree, gathering nuts, and could no longer move. The clan looked after him, feeding him, bringing him water for a season of days and nights, until one day he did not wake. Tye had been her age, and simply died. Mother said she coughed until her chest was empty of air. Uncle said she was called to the lights in the night sky. When the cave bear attacked, there were only the five of them left.

***

Father would stop on this hill to search the valley, for both danger and food. *But also, for something else,* thought Skeetu.

"Here, I feel all of the ground below me and all of the sky above," he would say. "Here, my Skeetu, I feel there is more than just us." His daughter felt the same. Since the cave bear, this had become even more of a special place. It was where she had buried Father's blackstone knife, something he had always carried with him.

Skeetu took a rest from hunting; she wasn't very hungry, anyway. She unwrapped the flute from the skin and played a tune. Some of it she'd learned from Owl. Some, from Yellowbeak. And some, most actually, she made up. The girl played until the sun began to dip below the tops of the trees. She would have to head back to her cave soon. Even with her spear, it was not safe to wander alone in the dark.

A rock flew past her head. Skeetu turned and saw three figures standing at the edge of the hilltop. One raised its arm and threw another rock, hitting her in the arm. Skeetu grabbed her spear and stood to face them. Her arm throbbed. They shouted something at her she didn't understand. The three moved closer and the girl could see them more clearly. Their skin was dark; their noses much smaller than any oldkin's. Their flattened faces wore angry-looking mouths. They were wrapped in mammoth fur—head to toe. One pulled back its hood. It was a girl; she could tell it was a girl, but a different kind from a different place. Her hair was black as a beetle's leg. The girl seemed to be studying her, too. She shouted again, making loud, chirping sounds—frightening sounds to Skeetu's ears. The sahaar picked up another rock and threw it at her. The oldkin ducked, but it clipped the top of her head. Her companions did the same and Skeetu ran down the hill, her screams nearly drowned out by the clacking of the stones landing around her!

It was dark when she returned to her cave. She could have made it back sooner, but she went around the long way, not wanting her tracks to lead the three to her home. As always, since the loss of her family, Skeetu threw stones into the mouth of her cave before entering, hoping to startle any cave bears that might have taken shelter while she was gone. All seemed quiet and she crawled inside.

"I do not like this new animal," she said, as she began to snap some branches into smaller lengths to awaken the sleeping fire. Then she stopped and laid down the sticks. It might be best to let the fire sleep right now. She rubbed her head where the rock had hit her. "No, I do not like them at all!"

Skeetu pulled some shriveled berries from a fold in the elk skin cloak she kept wrapped around her. As she chewed on them, she reached for the hare skin she'd rolled around her flute. It was kept tucked in her boot whenever she set out. *It is gone!* She frantically searched the floor of the cave and crawled out to look in the surrounding snow. It was nowhere to be found.

"It's up on the hill," she said to herself. But would it be there when she returned? *If* she was brave enough to return?

Chapter 5

Skeetu woke up in the morning, shivering. Normally, a fire would have kept her warm through the night, but she didn't want to risk being seen, or have the smoke smelled by the sahaar. *It should be safe now*, she thought, and built a small fire from yesterday's embers to warm her icy fingers. She reached into the hide wrapped around her foot, feeling for the flute. Of course it wasn't there, but it was an act done without thinking so many times in the past. Already, she missed greeting the morning with song. It had become a ritual, one she believed pleased those whose bodies could not be with her. She imagined them standing around the fire as she played for them, listening… smiling. Banor and Bint. Coughing Tye. Father. Mother. Uncle, and Bulo. It gave her strength to do what she must to greet another morning. And it made her feel less lonely.

"I will bring you back!" she shouted into the cold outside her cave.

The girl grabbed a bone from a pile she kept tucked on a rock ledge above her. It was from a hare she had speared two days ago. Her teeth scraped off the little bit of meat still stuck to it. Skeetu knew that the cold would let her keep food longer before it turned bad, especially if it was first burned in the fire. She didn't know *why*. It was just something that was. It had allowed her people to prepare for the fewer animals they could hunt during the long, white seasons. Of course this meant larger animals would be sniffing around her cache—cave lions, clawtooths, batbears, cave bears… all of them happy to make a meal of her. It was just part of life. Her life. She knew no different.

The oldkin had come home without food yesterday and would have to find some today. She picked up her spear and checked the stone point. It was sharp but would not be good for many more hunts. The black tree blood that held it to the stick still grabbed tightly. That was good. It was work to cook the blood of the whitetree to make it sticky. That had been Uncle's job, and then Bulo's.

Skeetu pulled the elk skins tightly around her shoulders and set off into the snow. She was going to Father's hill. With luck, her flute would still be there. With luck, the sahaar would not. Along the way she caught another hare. *Food for later. Might not even make it to the fire.* She tucked it under a flat rock to hide it from other hungry hunters.

When she reached the hilltop, she found neither flute nor sahaar.

"You took it! You took it!" she shouted, her voice echoing in the valley. She waved her spear in the air. "I will take it back!"

In the distance, where the valley opened up to flat land, Skeetu saw the heavy dark shapes of mammoths. One would feed her for a full moon cycle. If she could pull one down, which she could not. That took a whole clan. Then she saw one fall. She squinted her eyes, trying to focus on what she had just seen. Sahaar surrounded it, driving their spears into its side. Two more chased another, throwing their spears in long arcs. Skeetu laughed. *They waste their spears in the air!* She knew that to take down a mammoth, you had to face it to drive your spear into the killing spot. While she couldn't do it, or had not dared try, she had seen it done.

But their spears landed true! Both of them! Another mammoth fell.

"How do they do this?" she asked herself. "They send their spears like hawks to hunt for them!" She began to rethink the quest for her flute. The sahaar could kill from a long distance. She had a fresh hare waiting for her, and she was hungry. Skeetu started to turn back, but something made her change her mind. Part of it was the desire to get her flute back. But another part was a driving curiosity. What were these animals—the sahaar—in some ways like her, in some ways not?

She decided to follow them.

Chapter 6

Jen's dreams were overtaking her waking life. They began as short vignettes about her mother. They felt like memories, so clear, but ones she could not possibly have. The snippets of her mother's life advanced in reverse, her mother growing younger and younger, to the point where she was a child with *her* mother. Jen saw things both as her mother *and* herself, watching the scene. She felt a jolt seeing Mom in her mid-thirties. *Wow! That's me, right down to the short hair and bony elbows.* They shared the same proud nose that Mom always said came from a long line of "smelling the roses". When Jen woke, she felt strangely at peace. Her mother's love traveled through her slumber and nestled in with her.

The next night picked up where the previous left off. But now the subject was her grandmother. Gran began as Jen remembered her, a woman in her eighties, a bit ill tempered, always chewing on the inside of her cheek. Jen had done the same in her sleep. Gran was hunched and slow-moving, but Jen had seen pictures from when she was younger, showing her at a time when life was fully ahead of her. It was hard to tell the color of her hair from the old black and white photos.

But now she saw it was dark auburn, like her own. Then again, as the dream advanced, Gran became the younger version of herself. She was no longer a gran. Jen watched her raise her daughter, and then her son, Jen's uncle. Time flew in reverse to when her grandmother was a young girl being raised by *her* parents. She had seen her great grandmother once or twice when she was a very young child, but those memories were more like still photos than moving pictures. Now, in her dreams, her great grandmother came alive. And as with her mother, Jen felt a sense of love coming from her, from someone who only knew her as a child of three; it reached her now, thirty-three years later.

***

Night after night, Jen visited with people from her past. She no longer recognized who they were, but she knew they were her family, since their progression went straight from daughter to mother. They seemed to be connected by a single line, a genetic trait, which the archeologist was the last to receive. She had no children, or siblings. She was truly the end of this growing string of people. *I hope they're happy with where we all ended up,* thought Jen. *It all came to me.* While this was not particularly disturbing, the scientist in her needed to know why it was brought to her attention at this time. *Where are these people coming from? Did it have something to do with the flute on the nightstand?* The best place to start to unravel this mystery would be where it began, with her mother.

"How far back did your memories of me go?" asked her mother, as they sat at the kitchen table.

"To when you were a baby, in the hospital," Jen answered. She sipped the tea her mother always poured for her, even though she never wanted it. "No coffee, right?" she asked, as always, keeping the ritual alive.

"Nope," said her mother. "So, these memories can't be actual memories, can they? If you weren't there to see them, your dreams are filling in the story with your imagination. Dreams do that."

"Oh, I know that, but I have to tell you, it's pretty real-feeling! I mean… like when you were nine and you walked out to the porch and discovered someone had put mud in the mouths of all your dolls. You had them sitting in a circle, for a picnic."

"How would you know that? I hadn't thought about that in… forever! And I am sure I never told you!"

"See? Billy Shea was laughing just outside the doorway, and you caught him and called him a jerk. No, not jerk… monster, but you actually said *jonster*, because you were *thinking* jerk. And then you felt stupid for saying it, which made me—you—*us* even madder. You said you were going to tell his mother. He looked scared, but then tried to hide it and ran off. You saw the spoon he used to shovel the mud in the mouths, and you picked it up and threw it at him. Of course, you missed by a mile."

A visible chill ran through Jen's mother. "Jenny… you could not have known all of that! How did you… How would you see that… in a dream… or anywhere? I must have told you!"

Jen smiled. "Nope! Creepy, huh? This is what's kind of freaking me out. I see through the eyes of these women, and girls, in my dreams. Am I losing it?"

"Wait, what was I wearing?" asked her mother.

"If I told you, would you know if I was right? You would actually remember that?"

"I would. I was dressed for a party. With my dolls. Don't laugh. We were all young once."

"As I'm learning," said Jen. She closed her eyes and sipped her tea. "Blue dress, white shoes. The buckles in the shoes were uncomfortable. Dug into the tops of your feet."

"Oh, dear Lord!" said Mrs Moore. "Oh, dear Lord!" She stood up from the table and took a step back. "You're a psychic or something! I don't even believe in that stuff!" She looked at her daughter, concerned. "How long has this been happening?"

"Okay, sit down, Mom. I have another confession." Her mother hesitantly returned to her chair. Her palms pressed down on the table, bracing her for the next shock. Jen continued, "I stole something I should not have." She pulled the bone flute from her coat pocket. "This. It's a flute I discovered on a dig. I took it. Brought it home. *Stole it.* It breaks every rule in my profession, and I guess life in general—I've never done anything like this before. It's not *me*, but I guess it is because it's what *me* did."

"Why?" asked her mother. "I mean, no, it's not you!"

"*I don't know*!" said her daughter. "I don't know. It's like I had no control over it. I did it and I feel terrible. But it's when this whole dream thing started—this *psychic* stuff."

"Guilt?"

"Maybe. I mean, there's definitely guilt. But can that make me dream about things that I cannot possibly know?"

"Can I see it?"

"Yes, but be very careful. It's extremely fragile, and it's one thing stealing artifacts, it's another destroying them. I found this in a desert in Spain, in the hand of a Neanderthal girl."

Mrs Moore took the flute from her daughter's hand. Her fingers tapped at the holes in the side. "Hm…" she said. "How old is this?"

"About 40,000 years."

"Hm-hm-hmm… It's a flute? Have you tried playing it?"

"Can't. Look, it's filled with hard-pack sand. And I'm afraid cleaning it out will destroy it—collapse it. I think I have to try; I *know* I will, but it will be slow going. Can you imagine what it would sound like—after all this time?"

"Hm-hm-hmm," said her mother.

"That's it? Hm-hm-hmm…?"

"Hm-hm-hmm…"

Jen went to take another sip of tea, but her cup was empty.

"Another?" asked her mother.

"Sure."

Mrs Moore handed the flute back to her daughter, and then froze. "So… guess who just now popped into my head clear as day saying 'Hm-hm-hmmm', like she always used to. Mom—mine, my mom—your grandmother. I was right there with her. Or the other way around."

Jen stared at her, not knowing what to say. "This is just…"

"So, Jenny," her mother continued as she walked to the stove to grab the teapot. "Here we are. Either we're both crazy or…" She turned and nodded toward the flute in her daughter's hand. "We're not."

Chapter 7

The hunting party took down three mammoths. They removed the meat and organs with sharpened stones and wrapped them in the thick, hairy hides. They were then rolled onto large slabs of bark attached to long sticks and dragged by several of the sahaar across the plain.

Skeetu watched. She kept herself downwind, not knowing how strong their noses were, or how far her own scent would carry. The three girls who attacked her with rocks had been able to come upon her unnoticed. She would not let that happen again.

The oldkin followed the sahaar at a distance. They moved at a brisk pace, despite the burden they dragged behind them. The sun was directly above her by the time they disappeared in a narrow valley. *If I turn around now, I will be back at my cave before dark,* she thought. *With a fat hare for my belly.* But she had come this far. She crept to the rim of the valley and slowly peeked over the edge.

Skeetu took in a deep breath. Below stirred a large clan of sahaar. She looked at her fingers and then back down at the gathering.

"They are more than all the fingers on my hands," she whispered to herself. Some sat around a blazing fire, men, like the oldkin men she had seen in her short life. But also, not like them. They wore mammoth skins wrapped snuggly around their bodies. She looked at her elk skin cloak, simply draped over her shoulders. *How do their hides wind about their arms and legs?* The tall sahaar had a furry creature sleeping on his head! Or was it part of him? Skeetu ran her fingers through her long, wiry red hair. *I would like one for my own head.*

The hunters stumbled down the valley, dragging their catch behind. The clan rushed to greet them. They made noises Skeetu did not understand. They laughed, which was a sound she *did* recognize. It was a happy sound, much like that made by the oldkin, but it was higher; more like the young ground birds she'd hear in the spring.

Then she saw her. The girl who threw the rock! *She took my flute,* thought Skeetu. The other two were with her. They joined the rest of the sahaar as they leapt and sang in celebration of the success of the hunting party.

The oldkin watched. The excitement began to die down and most of the sahaar disappeared into openings in the tall, flat walls of the basin. The three girls stayed outside. They made laughing sounds and bumped one another playfully with their shoulders. Skeetu felt something new overtake her. It made her hate them, and not because of the rocks they threw. Or the flute they took. The three in the valley were as one in their joy. She had felt joy before. And she'd felt it many times in the company of her clan. *But these three are as one.* The oldkin had never been with a *she* of her age. There was only Bulo, but he was three summers older and a *he*. He was kind to her, and they found much to laugh about in the actions of their fathers, but he was not *just like her*. Skeetu looked down at the three girls, each just like the other. They walked along a thin rivulet that ran through the center of their dwellings. She followed from above, keeping her head low and footsteps silent. They stopped at a widening of the stream and sat in the low, soft grass. One pulled something from beneath her covering.

"My flute!" mouthed Skeetu. The girl in the valley put the flute to her mouth and played a tune for her companions. *What is she doing to it? It should not be making those painful sounds!* But she continued playing to the delight of the others. *She presses too many holes and blows through it like an old boar.*

Skeetu looked up at the sky. She would not be able to return home before dark. She'd have to spend the night on the edge of the plain. The girls in the valley got to their feet and began to walk back to join the clan. Skeetu glared down at them, angry that they took her flute. Angry that they made such ugly sounds with it. Angry that they threw rocks at her. And angry that they laughed as one. She picked up a rock and ran down the hill. It was dangerously steep, and her feet raced beneath her to keep her from tumbling forward. But Skeetu had run down many hills and was swift and steady as a longfoot hare. One of the girls saw her and squealed a warning. She was too late. The enraged oldkin struck the girl with the flute on the side of her head. The girl made no noise. Her knees collapsed and she fell, the flute dropping from her hand.

"That is mine! You took it from me!" shouted Skeetu. She grabbed the flute. The other two girls screamed and the sahaar burst from their holes in the rocks. The oldkin looked at the girl she'd hit with the rock. She lay as without life, blood spilling from her head. Skeetu looked at the other two girls.

"I did not mean to hit her so hard!" She held up the flute. "I just wanted to take this back!" They did not understand her and took a step back. A great noise came from the others and Skeetu turned and scrambled up the steep wall of the valley. Spears splintered on the rocks around her. She thought about the mammoths on the plain and remembered how the sahaar made their spears fly, but that's not what frightened her the most. A wailing rose from below. She knew that sound—sahaar, oldkin, it was the same. It was loss. Skeetu was overcome by a grabbing in her stomach. She felt ill. One did not take the life of one's kind. *But they are not my kind*, she thought. Still, she climbed faster. She made it safely to the crest and raced across the plain. The oldkin ran until there was no breath left in her chest and dropped to the ground. She rolled over and looked up at the twilight sky.

Skeetu sat up. She still held the flute and brought it to her lips. She wanted to make it sing again, but something didn't feel right—that grabbing in her stomach. She thought about the girl with the bleeding head. *Did I take a life to make these sounds?* It seemed that is just what she did. *But it's a sahaar!* Skeetu brought the flute to her lips, and then pulled it away. *But it* was *a life...* She thought about the girl's friends, wailing. They were in a moment not long ago, one in laughter, but now they were one less. *I need to hide.* The oldkin gathered her strength and went to stand. A searing pain shot up her leg. She looked down. A broken spearhead dangled from her calf.

Chapter 8

Shouts rose in the distance, growing louder. *Growing closer.* Skeetu peeled away the hide that was now pinned to her leg. The tough pelt had kept the spearhead from going in too deeply. She held her breath and gave it a quick pull.

"*Eeyaaa!*" she shouted in pain as the tip was freed. Her calf began to bleed heavily. She squeezed around the wound to hold it closed, which hurt even more. After a few trembling breaths, she eased up on her grip. The hole still bled, but more slowly. She stood and limped away. She could hear the sahaar coming closer and knew they would kill her if she didn't find a place to hide. The oldkin looked behind her, seeing a trail of red in the snow. Her blood would lead them right to her. Ahead lay the frozen river. It was her only chance.

The girl stepped onto the ice. It crackled beneath her feet. She shuffled, gently as she could, trying to make her body weigh no more than a leaf. *Soft, soft, soft,* she sang to herself in a whisper. *Soft, soft, soft…* The ice cracked some more, so loudly she was afraid the noise alone would lead the sahaar to her. She knew nothing about these creatures, except that they could easily hunt the great mammoths from a safe distance. *And that a stone could kill one as easily as one of my own.* The image of the sahaar girl she'd knocked to the ground clawed back into her head. That sick feeling returned to her belly. *I should not have done that!*

Skeetu was halfway across the river when the sahaar appeared at the bank. They were as many as fingers on her hand. They shouted things she could not understand—short, harsh hoots, yelps, and howls. But she knew what they meant. They would take her life for the one she took from them. *It is death by water or death by spear*, she thought, and raced to the other side. A spear pierced her elk hide, just grazing her own skin. Another whistled past her head. The ice cracked beneath her, and her foot splashed in the icy water, turning it instantly numb. She pulled it free just as a spear splashed in the hole she had made. The oldkin sprinted up the opposite bank, ignoring the pain in her leg, ignoring her frozen foot. With her spear held ready, she stopped to see what they would do next. The sahaar stepped onto the ice. They were all larger than her. *They will never make it across.* Another loud crack echoed over the frozen river and one of them fell into the water. He grabbed onto the spear of his companion and was pulled out. The angry men shouted at her from the bank, shaking their weapons in the air. They would not be able to cross.

Skeetu turned and scrambled up the hill. She found some moss growing at the base of a rock and pressed it into her wound. Her foot was still wet and cold, so she wrapped it with another clump of moss and sat on it until the feeling came back. She hunkered down, unmoving, as the moon replaced the low sun in the sky. She would have to spend the night in the open. It was dangerous, as much for the cold as the animals who hunted in the dark. Then she heard a sound back toward the river. It was a high, hollow whine.

"Bear? No… pig?" She quieted her breath so she could better hear. It called again, a stressful sound. "Not pig. Wolf cub?" The girl crept back toward the riverbank, spear in hand. *Do the sahaar make this noise?*

It was not a sahaar. A wooly rhino lay dead in the snow, a spear sticking from its unmoving chest. One of the spears that had missed her. A young one leaned against it, calling out in fear at the loss of its mother. It turned to face her, as if to charge and Skeetu got ready to jump aside. It had no full horn yet, but the beast was large enough to knock her down hard. And her leg hurt. And she was too tired to scuffle with a *spearnose* calf, especially one already heavier than a pack of Skeetus. She raised her weapon, ready to kill the animal, but then lowered it. This calf had lost its mother. She had lost her mother, too. While the sahaar girls had bonds that joined them as one, Skeetu felt a bond with this young beast.

She hummed a soft tune, "Hmm…. hmmmmm… hmmm…"

The rhino looked at her and then leaned against its mother. The fight had left its eyes. Skeetu slowly limped up to it, expecting it to run, hoping it wouldn't. She put her hand out to the frightened animal and touched its nose.

"I will not hurt you," she said. "I brought this spear to your mother. I am sorry." The calf huffed and lay down in the snow. Skeetu sat beside it and leaned back against the great wooly rhino, felled by a spear meant for her. It didn't feel right that it pulled the cold from her, but she took the warmth gratefully. She looked down at the young one, its head by her hip. "This was not a good day for us," she said. Skeetu pulled the flute out from her boot and held it to her face. "I do not want you any more. You put me here. A spear opened my leg because of you. I sleep in the cold against a dead mother because of you." She thought about the sahaar girl. "You made it throw rocks at me. You made me strike one down for you!"

Skeetu hurled the flute into the darkness. The calf was sleeping. The oldkin pushed into the fading warmth of its mother. She laid her spear across her lap and hummed quietly to herself to stay awake. It would be too dangerous to fall asleep with so many hunting for her—the sahaar and the hungry creatures she knew were out there. She was dreaming moments later.

Chapter 9

Jen walked around the Neandergirl site. She felt uneasy being here. It wasn't that she was alone, in a desert wilderness. Maybe that was it a little. It should be a concern for any woman or man out here, and it would be foolish to deny it. There were no rules or protocols broken in coming to examine a site on her own, especially one she had discovered. But she was doing so at the expense of plowing through the workload that waited at home. *I shouldn't have lied.* She had told her colleague she needed seven days off to deal with a family emergency. Private, she said. She tried to be vague as possible, knowing she would easily be tripped up if questioned, but Hirnhoff wasn't the nosy type. Plus, outside of his work, he didn't show much interest in her, or anyone else's personal life. Instead, he said, "Sure, go ahead. There'll just be twice as much work for you when you get back."

***

So she traveled to Spain, back to the desert. Back to her Neandergirl's home. *Lying is getting to be a habit with me. Along with grave robbing. What have I become?* In a way she *wasn't* lying. The site was where the dreams of her family began. There was, maybe not an emergency, but an urgency to learn what was shaking up her world. She knew the flute played a role in this, which was a very unscientific belief for a woman trained in the scientific method. But *as* a scientist, she could not ignore the hard evidence provided by her dream phenomenon. Evidence is evidence, even when it does not agree with your beliefs.

Jen knew there would be more to find here, as did her boss. They had planned on getting a larger team back to the site next year, when new grant money became available. She couldn't wait that long. She'd pay for this trip out of her own pockets, light as they were with funds.

In the months that had passed, her dreams brought her further back in history. She was now in the eighteen-hundreds. Their subjects still followed the lineage of her family, from daughter to mother. Last night, she was Sara Pendleton, a homemaker in 1835. Sara was her great-to-the-8th-factor grandmother. As always, she became that person; saw through her eyes; thought her thoughts. And yet, at the same time, she was herself, observing. She and her ancestors were, in a way, communicating in this separate, ethereal world.

While this would have driven many insane, Jen couldn't wait to go to sleep at night and see what old family member she would meet next. When she awoke, she jotted down what memories lingered, creating, if these were actual memories of things that occurred, a genealogical history. She wondered how far back this would take her.

"The answer is here, somewhere," she muttered, as she paced around the site. The edges of the excavation from last season were still marked with an outline of potato-sized rocks. The orange flagging was removed to keep this dig from being discovered by poachers. Theft was rare in these parts, and chances were miniscule anyone else would even come to this part of the desert, but it was always a good precaution.

The archeologist sifted through the outer borders of the section they removed. She was sure there would be something, a tool, a toe, a remnant of clothing, perhaps. She took the flute out of her backpack and unwound it from the bubble wrap that kept it protected.

"Here," she said to the ghost of Neandergirl. "Would you like it back for a bit?" Jen half expected to hear an answer, from somewhere, as she laid it down next to where the girl once rested. She had managed to pick a good amount of the hardened sand from the openings at both ends and had started working on the finger holes. She did it all by hand, not trusting the *finesse* of a motorized hand drill. There was still a long way to go before it would be completely cleared out.

The archeologist left that evening without having found anything new. She returned the next day and the day after that, and still came up empty. Each time, she placed the flute on the ground near where Neandergirl was found. She knew it was a silly ritual, bordering on superstitious, but her dreams had opened her mind to all possibilities.

***

On her last day, she further widened the search area, skimming in a growing circle around the site. The air was still, no breeze offered to temper the heat of the desert sun. She had to be more careful, both with dehydration and the yellow scorpions that hid beneath the rocks she turned. Their sting wouldn't kill her, she was told, unless she was allergic to the venom. At best, it would hurt, a lot.

There was only so much one person could cover and she was sure she was missing a world of things just beneath her feet. Then she came across something odd. *A shell?* She dug away some of the sand and it came free. *Big shell! Tusk shell maybe?* This didn't seem like the right place for one, too high in the strata. Neanderthals inhabited this land long after the sea had disappeared. Neandergirl's bones would be far above any remains of sea life. *Was this something traded from another clan?* Jen looked down at the spot where the shell was resting.

"Wait a minute!" She dug deeper, exposing more of the relic. "This is… going down… pretty… far." She looked over at the broken piece, and now realized that it was not a shell.

"Tip of the iceberg," she announced to the empty desert.

The archeologist dug for a few more hours. The sand had quickly become more compact and hacking through it was difficult. The intense heat wasn't helping. She was down two and a half feet, and the object was growing wider. Then she stopped and sat back on the edge of her trench. She was soaked in sweat and remembered to take a drink from her water bottle. The water was hot, but it kept her from passing out.

"You're a horn, aren't you?" she said to the thing in the sand. "Woolly rhino, I'm guessing!" Jen knew if that was the case, she was only a little more than halfway done digging. Woolly rhino horns could be over four feet long. It made sense to find one here. The three-ton beasts lived alongside the Neanderthals and early modern humans. The people hunted them. *Could this rhino have been the cause of Neandergirl's early demise?*

Jen looked around, making sure no one had seen her. It was just a habit. She was as alone as a person could be, but this site had just become more interesting yet. She didn't want anyone coming upon it, drawn by the obvious human disturbance she'd created.

"The plot thickens," she said. She reburied the horn but kept the tip that had broken off. *I'm already a thief,* she thought, *what's one more stolen artifact in my pocket?* The hardest part of this whole ordeal would now be keeping it a secret from Hirnhoff. She was exploding with the desire to share this, to discuss it with someone. But how *could* she tell him about this if she was supposedly back in the States with a sick family member? *I feel like I'm in high school, afraid to get in trouble with my teacher.* And in many ways Hirnhoff was her teacher. Much of what she'd learned came from the years working with him. He was often gruff with her, but that was his way. He was like that with everyone. Probably a little less so with her. But he'd never lied to her as she had to him. That she knew of…

Apart from the horn, the trip had yielded no new information. This was typical of fieldwork, but more frustrating than usual because of the personal connection she held with the subject. Plus, she had added yet another lie to the situation. Was there something to the new find—the horn she had reburied?

As Jen drove the rented Jeep from the desert, she tried to imagine her Neanderthal facing a charging woolly rhino. "No, that's not right," she said. "Why would it have died here with her?" Did they kill each other in battle? A twelve-foot long, six-foot high bulldozer with a jousting lance on its nose versus a four-foot, ninety-pound teenaged girl? Neanderthals were solid folk, powerfully built, but no match for a charging woolly rhino.

"Hm-hm-hmm," she said. "Now if that girl had a spear…" *It's possible they could have finished each other off,* she thought. But she also realized that they could have lived decades, even centuries apart. Bones don't always settle where they were first planted. *And this girl had a flute, not a spear.*

***

That night, Jen boarded her plane back to the States. It was an overnight flight and she dozed in her seat. She dreamed she was a young Ida Hestor, running to keep up with her father. Her father turned and shouted. He grabbed his daughter, inside whom Jen Moore now resided. Her sleeve tore as he yanked her into the grass. A horse-drawn cart rumbled just behind her and had nearly run her over.

"You *know* ya gotta be more careful!" scolded her father. Jen watched his anger soften. She could tell he was frightened for Ida, for *her*. "Yer all I got, kid. I won't always be there to yank ya outta the way o' things."

***

Jen woke up and went to brush the road dust from her knees. Then she realized she was still in a plane, and it was over a hundred and fifty years later. And that, woolly rhino or no woolly rhino, she was no closer to solving the mystery of her dreams. *The flute is in the baggage compartment below me, and it's still telling me stories.*

57

The plane landed early in the morning of the next day. Bleary-eyed, she followed the crowd through the gangway into the airport.

"Jennifer Moore?" asked a woman in a customs agent uniform at the gate. Another agent stepped behind her.

"Yes?"

"Will you come with us, ma'am?"

"What's wrong?" asked the archeologist.

"We need you to come with us," she said.

"Where?"

"We just have some questions. Hopefully, this won't take long, but we'll see," said the agent behind her. "This way please."

The two agents led her to a small, white room and took her bag and phone. They had her empty her pockets and patted her down. She was asked to remove her shoes, and she complied. She looked down at her dirty socks and was embarrassed. She had rushed to pack and hadn't planned very well. One of the agents inspected her shoes and handed them back to her. Jen tried to think of what she could have done. She had nothing on her that could have caused any concern. *Unless...*

"Did you pack anything in your bag that you know to be illegal?" asked the female agent. The other agent, a short, heavyset man, stood silently by the door with his arms crossed.

"Illegal? Like what?"

"Dinosaur bones?"

Jen laughed. "No! Not dinosaur bones. I'm not a fossil smuggler. I am an archeologist. I'm bringing back to my museum an old bird leg bone and part of a woolly rhino horn. If you look, you'll see my collector's permits in with the artifacts. I always do that, so they don't get separated. I also have a copy in my carryon bag."

She had lied about bringing them back to the museum, but she couldn't tell them the truth. Hearing the lie out loud gave her a twinge in her stomach. *This isn't me,* she repeated silently to herself. How many times would she have to say that to make it true?

"So here's what happened, and here's where we are," said the agent. "When your bag was X-rayed, the technician noted the presence of 'bones or something like it'. Of course, that's going to raise questions— bones in a suitcase. When we inspected the contents, we found the two bones, and the permit, and contacted your museum, as you did not list the items on your customs form. You could have been stealing them. The supervisor we spoke with said he knew nothing about either one of those items, and that he did not know you were bringing them back. Or that you were here, or in Spain. He sounded very confused. We needed to clear this up before we allowed you to leave with what could be contraband."

Jen felt the blood drain from her face. *He knows! Hirnhoff knows!* Could she go to jail for this? What had she gotten herself into? She thought quickly.

"Did you tell him I was bringing back *dinosaur* bones?" she asked.

"Yes," said the female agent, the only one doing the talking. Jen assumed the other one's job was to just look imposing.

"We aren't working on a dinosaur dig. Of course he's confused. I'm assuming you talked to my colleague, Dr Hirnhoff."

The agent checked her notepad. "Yes," she said.

"We are looking for *Homo sapiens* and *neanderthalensis*. They did not coexist with dinosaurs. The Flintstones got it wrong, you know." She smiled at the two agents, hoping to have lightened the mood a little. They returned her look with dead stares.

"Listen," Jen continued, "I have the collection permits for the site and for transporting artifacts. What I did *not* do, was label them, you are right. And yes, I failed to list them on my customs forms. I'm coming home from five days in a searing hot desert, on just a few hours' sleep. I slipped up on the paperwork. I'm sorry."

The two agents looked at one another. The one by the door nodded to the other.

"The museum contact was confused, but he said you are legit," said the agent. "We needed to make sure that you weren't smuggling illegal fossils. It does happen. In the future, though, you have to fill out the customs forms, listing *everything* you are bringing back with you from Spain. Or wherever."

"I will," said Jen. "Again, I'm sorry."

She filled out the forms, gathered her belongings and climbed onto the bus that would bring her to her car. She looked out the windows at the cold, dirty gray sky. *What have I done?* Jen's phone vibrated. She pulled it out of her pocket and read a message. It was from Hirnhoff, and read, "I guess we should talk?"

Chapter 10

Skeetu woke in the morning, trembling from a night out in the open. The dead rhino was cold as the air now and did little to keep her warm. The calf grazed on low plants where the snow had been blown away. It kept an eye on her, perhaps not trusting the oldkin, or perhaps not wishing to lose her. *It may not want to leave its mother,* thought the girl. She ran her hand down the hide of the great beast that lay dead. *This would hold me warm on the coldest nights. Bulo wore a spearnose hide.* Skeetu sniffed the animal. It didn't smell like Uncle's son. It smelled like… food. She looked back at the calf. *I cannot eat this beast in front of its young.* She grunted. *Oof, and I cannot take its hide.*

Her leg throbbed where the spear had pierced her, but the bleeding had stopped. She stood and looked around. The towering, orange grass spilled over a light blanket of snow on the plateau. The open sky sucked the warmth from beneath her feet and she stamped them to bring back feeling in her toes. At the far edge, tall needletrees formed a feathery wall of deep green. It would be warm in there. If it hadn't been for the shelter of the dead spearnose, it's where she would have spent the night. Although, she knew that inside that forest were clawtooth cats and packs of wolves. And other sharp-mouthed beasts hungry for small oldkins.

It was not the shelter of needletrees she looked for now. She searched the area for her flute and spotted it near where she'd slept. *What was in my thoughts? The bad things that happened were my own fault, and the sahaar's, not the fault of this singing bone!* But it was broken. It had hit a rock and splintered it into pieces. The heartache brought Skeetu to her knees. She rolled the fragments in her fingers. She could not make a new one but knew that she would try again. And if she *were* able to, it would never sound like this one had. The oldkin thought again about the sahaar girl. *She breathes no more over a thing I just tossed away.*

The girl stood and found the young rhino. She walked toward it, wondering if it would run from her. The calf stopped feeding and turned toward Skeetu.

"Are you going to charge me now?" she asked. Instead, it dropped its rump into the grass and sat, its body facing her, but with its head turned away. It made a defiant effort not to look at her but kept a subtle watch from the corner of its eye. The oldkin limped over to it. She gently rested her hand on its head. *Would a beast know a friendly touch?* The rhino did nothing. It continued looking away.

"What are we going to do now?" asked the girl. "Is it safe for me to go—" Skeetu froze. Something was here. She felt it in the sudden silence of the birds. Then she saw what had stilled them. It crouched low where the grass grew taller, the color of the grass itself. It was the eyes she noticed first, yellow like two suns. They were not looking at her, though, but at the calf.

"Clawtooth," whispered the oldkin to the young rhino. "Do not move." Skeetu slowly stepped away. Her spear lay on the ground by the dead mother, and she walked toward it. She kept her eyes on the cat. It would not move until it was ready to take what it wanted. Father had killed one once. She saw it dead, but still a thing to fear! It weighed more than all of them and had two great, long ripping claws in its mouth. The feet grew sharp, curved spears. One of those spears had torn Father's hide. It had been cut cleanly, as if by a freshly chipped blackstone knife.

"How did you stop this?" she had asked him.

"You have to want your life more than *it* does," he said.

"And stick it with a sharp spear!" added Uncle.

"Yes," laughed Father. "The sharp spear helps."

Skeetu reached her spear and bent to pick it up. Her eyes remained on the cat. She slowly stood and the young woolly rhino got to its feet and walked toward her. It seemed unaware of the danger behind it.

"No! Behind you!" warned Skeetu. The calf paused at the sound of her voice. The cat sprung from the grass.

"Yaah! Yaaaahhh!!" shouted the girl as she charged toward the beast. In her eyes it was all claws and teeth, driven by a fearsome wildness. It hit a patch of deep snow, which slowed it down, but not much. Skeetu

raced forward, forgetting about the hole in her leg. *I want my life more than it does!* The cat reached her and the oldkin thrust her spear at its face. She shouted at the top of her lungs, mostly in fear, but she had learned that, sometimes, loud cries will scare a beast away. It stopped and answered her in low rumbles she felt in her chest.

"*Yaah! Go! Go!*" she shouted. The cat was quick and dodged each jab of the spear, at times batting it away with a paw larger than her head. Then it stepped back, faced her and stood motionless. Those two yellow suns looked into the eyes of the girl. Now *she* stopped moving. The pause gave Skeetu a brief moment to realize what was happening. *This clawtooth will take my life. I* want *my life more, but it will take it anyway.*

The cat leaped in the air and landed on the girl. It held her down with one paw and snapped at her face. Skeetu had managed to grab the spear handle with both hands, and she pushed back against its throat. The cat's breath was thick and wet. It tipped its head to drive that great mouth-claw into her shoulder. The oldkin pounded the spear handle into its heavily muscled neck and heard the wood crack. She prepared for the next push to break it in half.

The ground trembled. Skeetu heard a dull rumble that grew louder. 'Thump-thump-thump-thump…' The cat heaved loudly and rolled off her. The rhino calf struck again. It had little horn to work with, only about as long as her foot, but it had hit the cat in just the right spot. *It is breathing out more than breathing in,* noticed

Skeetu. It struggled to get up. She slapped the spearnose on the flank to get its attention.

"We go! Now! *Now!*" she yelled and backed away from the cat. It was trying to get to its feet but was still struggling for breath.

"Come now!" shouted Skeetu and she ran across the plain. The calf followed. So did the cat, but without the will it had shown earlier. The oldkin turned to face it. The woolly rhino calf kept walking. The cat stopped and paced back and forth, considering another try at them. It roared; a sound that made the girl's knees grow weak with fear. She caught herself and straightened up. Then it turned and loped away. Skeetu leaned against a tree. She couldn't have moved if she wanted to. Her body shook as if bitten by the teeth of an icy river. She waited for her breaths to steady.

The rhino kept walking. It headed toward the forest, where the edges were free of snow. Skeetu knew it would find plants to eat there. She had seen only a few spearnoses before. They grazed like aurochs and elk in the open spaces. The oldkin drew in a long, calming breath and set off in its direction.

Uncle told stories of woolly rhinos he'd heard from other clans; they were all stories of loss; speared or trampled by a "spearnose", as he called them. They were as dangerous as the mammoths, maybe more since they were quicker and less patient with challengers. There were only a few of them, though. Too rocky here. Bulo had found a dead one three winters ago, taken down by wolves. The animals had no use for the hide, so he waited for them to finish their meal and took it for himself.

Skeetu looked at the calf trotting ahead of her. She jogged to keep up. She wasn't sure how much further she wanted to go in this direction, but at least it was away from the clawtooth. *This one defeated a clawtooth and it is just a young one, with a bump of a horn.* Skeetu could not imagine herself going up against one the size of this one's mother. Her horn was as long, or longer than the oldkin's height, wider than her at its base, and harder than a nut tree's wood.

Then she remembered. She had to get back to her cave. The embers in her fire pit needed to be fed their sticks or they would die forever. Skeetu clapped her hands to get the rhino's attention. It ran a little further and then slowed and turned its head back toward her.

"I have to go home," she shouted. "I will come back to see you!" The calf continued to look at her. Skeetu worried about the animal, alone, with no mother to protect it. She could not stay here with it, though.

"Watch for clawtooths!" she warned. The oldkin turned to head back to the river. She knew of a place further downstream where she would be able to cross the ice safely. Then she felt the ground thumping beneath her feet. She turned and saw the calf, running to catch up with her.

"No, no, no," said Skeetu. "My home is not a place for you!" She tried pushing it away, but it might as well have been a mountain. "Okay, come with me, then. We saved each other once. Maybe we will do it a second time." Her hand fell on the beast's back, and she rubbed the thick wool. "It is like Bulo's cloak." She smiled. "I will call you Bulo."

Chapter 11

Skeetu made her way back to her cave. The cold seasons lingered long and curling up near a bed of warm coals at night would help her get through it. There were few lightning storms during this bleak time, so she could not count on finding new embers in trees clawed by its glowing fingers.

Bulo followed, often at a distance. He stopped frequently to clear patches of low plants from the ground. *You are always warm,* thought Skeetu, looking at his woolly coat. *Maybe you could keep me warm at night. If you do not roll over and crush me.* She didn't wait for him. He always managed to catch up on his own. *Does he think I am his mother now?*

She reached the part of the river where she hoped to cross. It was shallower here, a place she would come to in the warm season to spear fish near the surface. It was now covered with thick ice. Skeetu crossed easily and waited on the other bank.

"Bulo! You be careful," she called out to the calf. "Walk like a you are a feather." The rhino clomped onto the ice, and it cracked beneath his weight.

"No! You are too heavy! Go back!" shouted the girl. Bulo trotted across, the ice breaking apart behind him as he went. He fell through just before reaching the other side. She was about to jump in to help when the rhino waded through the water and stepped out.

"Oh. You can swim," said the oldkin. Bulo snorted and continued on his way. It happened to be where Skeetu was heading and now she ran to catch up with *him*.

They reached her valley just before dark. They had made a quick detour to pick up the hare she stashed away the day before. That seemed so long ago! Her cave was a short distance ahead. Skeetu stopped. She smelled smoke. She looked for fire in the trees, but none around her were burning. But that didn't mean they weren't burning elsewhere, and that the fire couldn't travel quickly to overtake her. The oldkin rushed to her cave. It would be the safest place to ride it out. Then she saw something glowing inside the entrance. *Did my embers wake on their own?* No. The flame was moving, dancing on the end of a stick. It was carried by—

"Sahaar!" she said to herself. Bulo lumbered up behind her. The oldkin turned and pushed him back with both hands. The rhino stopped, but only because he chose to. Another fire stick appeared inside her cave.

"We can't go here," she whispered. *They found my home!* She would wait the night out in a small, nearby cave. The sahaar wouldn't think to look for her there, as the entrance was hidden behind a thick growth of rippershrub. She knew how to crawl low at the base, which was free from the hostile spikes.

The oldkin reached the shrub before the moon rose too high to reveal her to the hunting sahaar. She was about to crawl under when she realized Bulo would be unable to follow. *He won't be safe out here,* she thought. *If the sahaar don't get him, there are other things that will.* She stood and pushed the young woolly rhino toward the outside wall of the cave beside the bush. Again, the pushing did nothing, but maybe suggest to the beast the girl's intent. He moved on his own and leaned against the rock.

"Stay here, Bulo. Sleep here. Do not move! Do not move!" pleaded the girl in urgent whispers. The rhino looked at her. Skeetu could see he didn't understand. How could he? She pushed down on his back.

"Down. Lie down! Sleep here. I will be in that hole right next to you." The calf seemed to decide that lying down was something he wanted to do. He sat and then rolled onto his side. Skeetu had an idea. She snapped off some branches from a nearby bristletree and piled them atop the animal. Aside from lifting his head to watch what she did, Bulo remained still. *He will be a little harder to see now. And the smell of the branches might hide his own.*

"Good, Bulo! Please stay. Do not make noise. Do not move until I come out." The girl sighed. *He won't stay.*

Skeetu pushed under the rippershrub and used her elbows to carefully drag herself forward. The thorns were sharp and would slice deeply. Those who were cut sometimes grew very ill around the wound. She made it to the entrance unscratched. It was dark within, but light of the rising moon snuck in through a wide crack near the ceiling. The high squeaks of bats told her she wasn't alone. They came and went in the dusk, dark, fluttering shapes, paying her no mind. The oldkin shivered in the cold. She was wishing for a fire when she heard noises outside. Skeetu crawled to the back wall of the small cave. It was too low for her to stand. She'd left her spear outside! She got to her knees and felt for a rock to use as a weapon. There was a crinkling of leaves by the opening and a dark figure slipped in past the rippershrub.

"Bulo!" She scuttled over to him and ran her hand down his hide. It was too thick with heavy fur to be pierced by the thorns. The rhino settled in against the wall and was quickly asleep. Skeetu nestled in next to him, much preferring the warmth of her young friend to that which kept her warm the night before.

***

In the morning she crawled out of the cave. A light snow had fallen overnight. *Good, I will be able to see if they left.* Bulo pushed through the shrubs and bumped past her, eager to find something to eat.

"I'm going to my cave," said the girl. "You should stay here." The rhino brushed the snow away with his muzzle and picked at the low grass with his teeth.

Skeetu crept away. When she reached the cave, she saw by the sahaar footprints that they'd left. She went inside, hoping none had stayed behind. No one was there. The oldkin rushed over to the pile of ashes that had held the embers and brushed them aside. She could feel the warmth in the fine dust and breathed a sigh of relief.

"They are still alive!" The air ignited the tiny nuggets, and they began to glow. She fed them small sticks, blew on them, and they grew into flames. Skeetu built the fire up high. She needed to make more embers. They would have to travel with her now. The sahaar would be back and she could no longer stay here. Once she'd brought the fire back to full life, she'd cook the hare and then let the flames die down. It would leave behind its sleeping children.

Skeetu enjoyed the warmth of the fire. She was tempted to spend the day here. It was restful. It was home. But she knew she could not. The oldkin went outside and found an old bird nest. She made a handle by tying thin vines to the woven edges. When the fire died, she lined the nest with a heavy layer of ashes, and then dropped some glowing embers on top. These were buried with another layer of ash, which was then covered with a strip of elk hide to protect the contents from rain and snow.

***

The girl left her home, the only one she had ever known, and set out to find Bulo. She didn't have to look very long, as he came trotting up to her. His face was caked in snow from foraging for plants.

"Will you come with me?" asked Skeetu. "I think I will go to the needletree forest back on the plain. At least until the nights are warmer. And we'll be better hidden." The rhino's gentle brown eye watched her beneath lashes coated in ice. Looking into Bulo's eye was different from looking into the eye of another beast or bird. *They* just *watched* you. The oldkin would sense them wondering how much longer they should freeze before running off. It was not so with the calf. Bulo looked at her as if he knew who she was. He was here. She was here, and it was how it would be because it was what they both wanted. It lifted the girl's mood, and despite all that had happened to her, she smiled at the beast. Her protector. Her companion. A clawtooth lived by the forest. Wolves no doubt ran through the darkness beneath its branches. Hungry batbears prowled. But she was no longer alone.

Chapter 12

"So, what now?" asked Jen. She sat across her boss in his cluttered office. He looked hurt. Angry would have been better. She told Dr Hirnhoff the entire story, leaving nothing out. *The lying is over,* she thought. It was a relief but hearing her own words describing her deeds hit her harder than anything Hirnhoff could say to her.

"Well, you can start by returning the two items," he said. Jen opened her bag and laid the chunk of woolly rhino horn on his desk.

"Found this last trip. It's only the tip. The rest of it is buried pretty deep. Got only a couple feet down."

"And the flute?"

"Oh, Stan, I can't give that to you. I'm sorry. I just can't."

"Jen, it doesn't belong to you. It doesn't even belong to our museum! It is the property of the Spanish government. I'm fairly certain you know that! You're the one who files all the paperwork. Anything and everything we uncover is only on loan to us, with the agreement that we share any information we have with Madrid. Should they choose to call it back home, we would have to return it."

"I know. I know! Do they know about it?"

"Not that I am aware of," said the professor.

"Stan, there is something very strange going on here. I have some kind of connection with that artifact. As I said, something about it is pulling me through my dreams! I'm learning things that I could not possibly know otherwise."

"Just you? Let's test it. Would it work on me?"

"I don't know. But I don't think so. I cannot imagine anyone else having the personal connection I have with this thing. Although my mother felt it, too — odd…"

"Your mother knows about this?"

"I had to talk to someone, and, well, it obviously couldn't be you… It's part of my soul, Stan! I *know* I sound crazy! It is so hard to hear myself say these things! But I don't think I am."

"No," said Hirnhoff, looking somewhat sympathetically in her eyes. Jen would have preferred any look but that one, which suggested he thought she was deluded. "Nothing of the kind is happening! You may be having vivid dreams, but there is no conceivable way and old bird leg is driving it! Do you hear yourself? There is no logic to it! This is not the woman I know. If you are having problems with sleep, or your love life, or anything like that, we can get you help. You must return it. It's not even a question!"

"My love life? What are you even talking about?"

"I don't know. I'm just throwing stuff out there. I'm not used to this. This isn't my job, corralling rogue scientists."

"I cannot return it," said Jen. "I physically can't. It won't let me."

"Oh, come on! You can't be serious. Where is it? Do you still have it?"

"I do."

"Listen, not only have you stolen from the Spanish government, but you also have in your possession something that dramatically changes what we know about *neanderthalensis*! It's a missing link. A link between the creative brain and the primitive brain of an intelligent hominid that came to the end of its line! If you found this flute in the girl's hand, it settles the question once and for all about whether or not *neanderthalensis* had the capacity to… not only create music, but to create the tools to produce it! Does this mean they could create visual art as well? That's not a far step from making musical instruments. In fact, I'd say that would likely come first."

"She could have found it."

"Yes, she could have. But without the actual artifact to study, we won't have the opportunity to piece this together."

"Yeah, in a year from now," said Jen.

"Oh, come on! You know this would get jumped on right away! Why are you even arguing with me, Jen? You know what you have to do! Who *are* you? This conversation—this situation—is unreal!" Hirnhoff's face was turning red. Still, despite his distress, Jen could not back down.

"I know. But then what? Something this important will eventually be taken back by the Spanish government. Stan, I can't give it up! Yet. Not yet. I'm sorry! So knowing that, what happens now?"

Dr Hirnhoff pushed his chair back and stood. He looked down at his colleague, who was on the verge of tears. Then he picked up the woolly rhino horn and looked at it more closely.

"This was at the site, yes? *Coelodonta antiquitatis.* Not exactly rare."

"Yes. About forty feet from Neandergirl—um the *neanderthalensis*." She realized Hirnhoff was already questioning her sanity, and her unnatural connection with the bones they found.

"Hm. Could have a lot of explanations. Return the flute, Jen. This is the last time I am telling you this. Return the flute. Then we'll get you some help."

"With my love life?"

"Oh stop. I was sputtering."

Jen stood up to face the professor. She wasn't angry with him. In fact, she knew he was one hundred percent right, about everything. She would have demanded the same from any intern, and then fired him or her.

She took a deep breath, and then said, "I cannot. Am I fired?"

Now Hirnhoff took a breath and said, "Yes, Jen. I'm afraid so. Why you have done this to me, I'll never know."

"No, no, Stan. I completely understand. I've given you no choice. I will gather my things and leave. I really am so sorry I'm doing this to you. And for lying to you! That was the worst part for me! You don't deserve it."

"You know, when I hired you straight from the university six years ago, I did so because I saw in you a talent I had seen in no other."

"Ten years ago," corrected Jen.

"What? No, not ten years." He thought a moment. "Okay, maybe. Anyway, you have an eye for fieldwork. You can spot an *Australopithecus* molar from a mile away. In time, you would have been running the research department here, or anywhere in any facility you wanted! You are that good! It is a crime you have thrown this away—and by committing a crime! And how will I find someone like you? Have you thought of that?"

"Those are the nicest things you've ever said to me in the ten years I've known you."

"Yeah, well it's not going to help anything, is it."

"No, I'm afraid not," said Jen.

"You will still need to return the flute."

"What if I am unable?"

"Ugh… Are you really going to make me say it, Jen? After all these… *ten* years? After all we have accomplished? I know I'm no teddy bear, but haven't I always been fair to you?"

"You have," said Jen. "Are you saying you're going to the police?"

"Please don't let it come to that, but you're putting the whole museum in jeopardy. Jen, you stole from us! And bear in mind that if you are convicted, you will be separated from the artifact for as long as you're in… just don't make me do this. Please."

"Can you give me some time, Stan? Madrid doesn't know about it, so it's not like they're going to be putting pressure on you. And I'm surely not going to let anyone know about it. I promise I will not put the museum in jeopardy."

"You've already told your mother!"

"My mother understands the seriousness of what I've done. She would never do or say anything that would bring harm to her daughter. Can you give me a couple days to sort this out before you call the police on me?"

"Forty-eight hours, and no more."

"Thank you, Stan."

"If you were truly appreciative, you wouldn't make me do this. Do *not* make me do this, Jen! I would consider it a cruel act upon me, by you."

"You just don't understand. And there is nothing I can do to change that. I'm sorry. And thank you. For everything. I mean it, Stan. This is not how you deserve to be repaid for all you have done for my career."

Jen left the office. She knew she would be fired; there could be no other course of action for what she had done. She also knew there was a chance, things would escalate beyond that. *I could hide it until I got out of jail. But what of my dreams during that time? Am I actually going to be in prison? Is this something you go to jail for?* It was a hard thought to wrap her mind around. Her dreams were now traveling through the fourteen hundreds. Daughter to mother, daughter to mother, as always, without a single break in the lineage. Despite Hirnhoff's belief to the contrary, the flute *was* the connection. Her mother felt it, too. And despite his insistence it be returned, she was powerless to do so.

She arrived in her apartment and called out to Dugg. The German Shepherd trotted up to her from the other room, his tail wagging recklessly. Jen bent down and hugged him, enjoying the only good feeling she'd felt all day.

"Ahh, Dugg… Things are going to be very different for now on. For you and for me." She stood and walked into the kitchen and opened the cabinet below the sink. Hidden inside an empty detergent box was the flute, and she pulled it out. She thought it best to keep it hidden, just in case. Although she really didn't know what that *just in case* was. *Police, maybe?* The crane leg bone was still partially packed with hardened sand in the center and would take more work to clear it out.

Jen walked into the other room and sat in front of her computer. There was much to do, and only two days to get it done. *First thing's first*, she thought. She opened up the travel site and booked a flight back to Spain.

Chapter 13

Three winters passed. Skeetu and Bulo had settled on the edge of the deep forest where the open land met the trees. The woolly rhino had grown considerably. His head was now at the height of the oldkin's. She had to stand on her toes to reach up to scratch him between his shoulders. The great horn was longer than she was; the smaller horn behind it, as long as her arm. Bulo had grown attached to the girl and generally went where she went. Sometimes it was the other way around, as Skeetu was curious about where he would lead her. *Maybe to other spearnoses,* she thought, although she was afraid of what would happen if he did come across another of his kind, especially another male. But a patch of succulent greens was always at the end of his trail. While she had come to trust the rhino, he did have a dangerous side. On occasion, and without warning, he would suddenly break into an outburst of wildness. This was a concern to the girl as he ran in circles, snorting and panting, driving his horns into unseen targets. In those moments, he was blind to the oldkin, and probably to anything else around him; she knew he would not intentionally hurt her. But she knew that to avoid him charging right over her, she had to be ready to sprint to

83

safety at the onset of his spells. After a few rampaging circles, he'd settle down to his gentle self, seemingly unaware of what had just happened.

The hunting was good for Skeetu. Food was plentiful. She had made a cozy shelter of soft needletree branches, leaning them across a beam formed by a partially fallen tree. It kept her dry and cradled the warmth of a small fire. Bulo had tried to join her inside on several occasions, his horn nearly tearing down all her work. He was forced to settle for sleeping outside, next to the shelter. He was unbothered by the cold anyway. He seemed unbothered by much of anything. *Do you remember your mother*, she wondered? *Do you still see things you wish you could stop seeing?* Skeetu wished that he did not. She wondered, though, if his attacks at the air had something to do with that terrible night.

Wolves were a problem. They would surround her home to feed on the scraps of bones and hardmeats Skeetu tossed aside. When they ventured too close, Bulo chased them off. He became a different animal when he was defending their home, similar to when he went into his circles of rage, but more focused. He appeared to see nothing but the beast he was chasing. Again, the oldkin knew enough to give him room, but she also knew it would take just one wolf to injure him, and the others would quickly take advantage of his weakness. It was just a matter of time. She solved the wolf problem, somewhat, by trekking far from her shelter to throw the scraps in the river, where they would be washed away. Still, one wolf stayed at the edge of her camp. It was always there. It didn't come close enough to be a threat, maybe because of Bulo, but maybe not. The rhino had long stopped showing concern, so she worried less about it.

They were in a time of warmer days. Plants grew, flowers bloomed, birds sang. The biting insects had awakened hungry, as they did at the onset of every high-sun season. It always took Skeetu a while to relearn to ignore them.

"Are you coming?" she asked Bulo. "Or are you just going to stay here and eat all day?" The rhino took a bite of grass and stared at her blankly, chewing. She was going to the sahaar valley. She had been there once before since that first time, and watched them from the edge. One of them saw her and raised alarm, but Skeetu was strong and fast. They could not catch her, or Bulo. She liked being chased. *They can fly their spears like hawks, make fire with stones, but they cannot catch a swift little oldkin.*

Skeetu set out for the valley. Bulo had decided to join her and wandered behind at his own pace. She had learned a faster way to reach the sahaar. If she followed the riverbank, it brought her to the lip of their basin. She could walk along the edge and see anyone coming long before they would see her.

The oldkin and her spearnose reached the valley by late afternoon. She stopped and ate some berries while

Bulo's lips plucked some fat leaves from a patch of mud.

"Wait," said the girl. "Do you hear that?" *Humming. Sahaar?*

"Over there," she whispered to Bulo, shoving him behind some boulders. By now, the rhino had learned to read what Skeetu wanted, and responded, as always, after appearing to think about it a moment. The oldkin ducked in next to him. The sahaar continued along the edge of the canyon, humming to itself. It carried a spear and had a sack hanging across one shoulder. Its coal black hair was long, down to its waist, and was bound tightly in a strip of hide. Its face—

"It's her!" said Skeetu. It was the girl she thought she had killed! She was alive! The oldkin found herself short of breath as a flood of joy washed through her. *I did not kill this sahaar!* She stepped out from behind the rock.

"Wait!" she called out. The sahaar froze, and then turned and ran. Skeetu quickly caught up with her and tackled her to the ground. She held the girl's wrists as she tried to throw the oldkin off her. Skeetu was much stronger than her, though. She just wanted to make her know that she was sorry for what she had done.

"Do not fight me!" she shouted. The sahaar, not understanding the loud words coming from her captor, fought back harder. She shouted something, using sounds Skeetu did not recognize.

"I am sorry for what I did, sahaar! I thought I sent you to the lights in the sky! I want you to know I am happy I did not!"

The sahaar stopped fighting. Maybe it was something in the oldkin's expression that told her this was not an attack. Maybe it was the pleading sound of her voice. Skeetu eased her grip. The two of them searched each other's eyes, trying to read meaning beyond the words neither understood. The sahaar said something, more quietly.

"I wish I knew what you say," said Skeetu. "I wish—"

The girl on the ground looked past the oldkin and called out. Skeetu was kicked in the shoulder by a larger sahaar. She rolled and stood up. The sahaar was a male. He was young, his face was clean, unlike those of the others she saw with fur-covered chins. He looked a lot like the girl she had tackled—same eyes, same shaped face and nose, same beetle-black hair. He waved his spear at the oldkin. Skeetu noticed it had two red feathers tied below the base of the point. The other sahaar called out to him and grabbed his arm, but he shook free and walked toward Skeetu. The ground began to tremble, and Skeetu knew what that meant. The faces on the two sahaar showed that they now knew, as well.

"Down the hill!" she said. "Run down that hill!" But they were not listening to her. They were too busy staring wide-eyed at the charging woolly rhino. The girl looked at the oldkin and shouted something, as if in warning.

"No! Run!" shouted Skeetu, "He won't hurt me!" The male started to lift his spear and changed his mind. The two ran down the steep side of the valley. Bulo slid to a stop just before the edge. Skeetu watched as they disappeared down the hill. She was disappointed, and her shoulder hurt, but she'd be all right.

The oldkin turned and stroked Bulo's fur.

"Thank you," she said. "Please do not hurt the girl, if we see her again. The other one?" She rubbed her shoulder. "Yes, you can run him down."

The next morning, Skeetu left for the sahaar valley. She went without Bulo. The oldkin had a feeling the sahaar girl did not want to hurt her and the spearnose would just scare her off. If the male were there, too, she would run. She was stronger than he was, maybe, but she did not want to hurt any more sahaar.

She did bring her spear, though. It was always with her, but that had less to do with the sahaar than with the other beasts that roamed. In her other hand, Skeetu held a rolled hare skin. It contained the broken fragments of the flute. Many days and nights were spent trying to repair it, but she could not. She would offer what was left of it back to the girl. It was hers. Even when Skeetu had found it, it was hers. The girl had probably dropped it. Or left it behind after sitting on her hill. *I do not like that she was on Father's hill though,* she thought.

Skeetu waited behind the rock for the girl to come. She heard humming in the distance. The oldkin's heart beat faster. *She is humming so I will hear her!* She peeked around the rock. The sahaar was alone. She appeared to be looking around. *Maybe for me?* Skeetu took a breath and stepped out from her hiding place. The girl stopped and the two stared at each other. She said something.

"I do not know what that means," said Skeetu. The sahaar squinted her eyes and looked past her. She repeated what she said before, but this time held the end of her spear up to her nose.

"Bulo! No, he is not here." Skeetu pushed the air behind her, as if she were pushing her spearnose friend away. The sahaar looked relieved. She said something else and motioned toward her head, where the oldkin had struck her a time ago. Skeetu looked down, ashamed. Then she remembered the broken flute. The oldkin laid her spear on the ground and took a few steps toward the girl. She held out the hare skin. The sahaar did not step back, and laid down her spear, too. She stared at the thing in the other's hand. Skeetu dropped to her knees and unrolled the skin. She patted the broken bones and then gestured toward the sahaar.

"Take this back. I am sorry I broke it. It is yours." The girl looked at the shattered pieces. She appeared puzzled, but then smiled. She made a sound that Skeetu liked. The sahaar rolled the bones back into the skin, stood, and tucked them in her pouch. She smiled and patted her chest.

"Haana," she said, "Haana. Haana."

Skeetu repeated, "Haana. Haana."

The girl patted her chest again, saying more emphatically, "Haana! Haana!" Then she reached out to touch Skeetu. The oldkin recoiled, and then felt foolish. She leaned forward so the sahaar could touch her shoulder.

Instead, the girl touched her own chest one more time and said, "Haana." Then she gestured toward the oldkin.

"*Oh!*" said Skeetu. "You are Haana! You are called Haana!" She grabbed the front of her own cloak. "Skeetu! I am Skeetu!"

"Skeetu," said the girl, with a wide smile. She reached into the pouch that hung from her shoulder and handed something to the oldkin. "Skeetu," she said again.

The oldkin held it in her hands, unable to speak. It was another flute! It was just like the other one, maybe a little smaller, but it was a flute! She did not know what to say.

"Skeetu," said the sahaar. She turned, picked up her spear, and trotted back toward her home. Skeetu stood there, still staring at the flute.

"Why did you give me this?" she shouted.

"Skeetu," the girl shouted back.

Skeetu looked down at the flute. "Haana," she said.

Chapter 14

Skeetu and Haana met often throughout the high sun season. At first, they mostly communicated with hand gestures and eager sounds. In short time, they learned each other's language. One of the first things Skeetu learned, at least as best she could, was the meaning of *sahaar*.

"I am sahaar to you," said Haana. "You sahaar to me. We sahaar to sahaar."

"What does it mean?"

The girl thought a moment, searching for a way to explain with the limited words they shared. "Sahaar is… ones we do not know. But it is also ones we know."

"A stranger, and a… friend? They are two different things in one word," said Skeetu.

"Yes. A strange one. You *were* sahaar to we… me. And a… friend. We are sahaar now. It is how we say and… how we *hear* the word that make them different."

"All begin as sahaar until they are not any more," said the oldkin. "And then they are again." It made no sense to her; both meanings sounded the same in her ears, but Haana nodded in agreement. She and the girl were mysteries to one another. They looked different, sounded different, even smelled different, but there was much about them they shared. They walked on two legs, like the birds. They had hair on their heads, like the mammoths. They hunted, like the wolves. They fished, like the bear.

Skeetu could not visit Haana's people in the valley. The sahaar girl told her she would likely be attacked, so their time together was spent in the oldkin's forest. It was safe for them there. If Haana were to be seen with an oldkin, she would be punished. Her people feared them, believing they brought bad luck. Only her brother Rin knew about her visits. While he was mute, he could find other ways to share his thoughts, but he chose to keep Haana's secret. Sometimes he would walk with her to where they met, but he'd turn back once they set out for Skeetu's home.

"Why does he not come?" asked the oldkin.

"He does not like Bulo," said her friend.

"Bulo won't hurt him. He knows Rin won't harm me."

"I have told my brother this," said Haana. "He also does not like you."

"Because I am oldkin?"

"Not only because that. He remembers this." The girl pulled her hair aside to show Skeetu the scar on her head. "I do not remember, but he does."

"I know you have said you do not remember when I hit you with the rock. But I still do not understand this. You should remember better than anyone. Except me."

"I forget things," said Haana. "Ever since… the rock, I am told. I remember that you told me why you did it. I remember I threw rocks at you. And took back my flute. But after that…"

"I did not want to send you to the lights in the sky. I did not think anything like that. I just knew I wanted my—your—flute back. I do things when I think of them. I am learning to think of things *before* I do them. When I thought I killed you I felt my insides turn to bumpy water. I—"

"I know. We both should learn to stop hitting others with rocks," said the sahaar. "Rin saw you attack me. It is harder for him to forget. He thought I went to the deep valley."

"Where is the deep valley?"

"It is like your *lights in the sky*. When we breathe our last, we go to the deep valley. It is a deepness beneath all valleys."

"Have you seen it?"

"No. But in a time before Father's father, a man fell into it. His brother watched this and cried out. His cry traveled over and over, across the valley, repeated by the wind. He saw the falling man—his brother—grow smaller and smaller. Then he grew so small he could not see him at all. The falling man's brother returned and told his clan of this. He told them his brother now hunts with the people who have fallen there before. The man's falling brother showed us where we all will go."

"All who are now gone, are in that valley? They all now hunt together?"

"Yes, Skeetu. They hunt and share great horns of slow-water with those who went before them."

The oldkin thought about this. She imagined Mother, Father, Uncle and Bulo, stalking hare and elk with Banor and Bint. They would sit around fires and the ancient ones would tell tales from the far circles of winters and summers.

"Haana?" she began, hesitantly. "Do the *oldkin* fall to this deep valley? We are told we rise to the lights in the sky, like sparks from a sticky-tree fire."

The sahaar looked away as she pondered this. Then she met her friend's eyes. "I do not know," she said. "I have not heard it said that you do *not*. I wish that you do. But if you do not, you still have your sticky-tree sparks in the sky."

Skeetu smiled.

"But that is why Rin does not like you," continued Haana. "He did not want me to fall into the deep valley."

"We are both glad you did not," said the oldkin.

The wind picked up and the two went further into the shelter of the forest.

"Oh. I forgot to tell you. I *think* I forgot… Maybe I did not. Dami and Soohla now know about you—about us," said Haana. They sat on a stone by a bubbling creek, crunching on mudbugs. Bulo grazed on the succulent leaves along the edge.

"Did *you* tell them?" asked Skeetu. "Did you not say no one could know about me? And us?"

"I have told you, Skeetu. Everyone *knows* about you! We have all heard of the red-maned oldkin spirit who wanders outside our valley with a great spearnose. For some, you bring fear. For others, *more* fear. When the night comes, Bravah, our old one, offers words for you to hear. Do you ever hear them?"

Skeetu laughed. "You have told me this. I don't know if I hear them. I am not what you call a *spirit*, so how can I? But I do hope they still believe it true!"

"Most do," said Haana. "You have met Dami and Soohla." The sahaar looked uncomfortable. "They were with me when we chased you with rocks?"

"Yes, you have said their name. How do they know you are my friend? Rin?"

"No, Rin would not open that secret. He looks out for this one. He is two summers older, but he protects me like he is Father. Except when Bulo is nearby. Then he hides like baby Momo. *I* told the two about you. I think it was safe to do this. They won't open that secret, either."

"Bring them next time," said Skeetu. "But I will hide all the rocks first."

They went back to the shelter. There was a chill in the air. The oldkin built up the fire.

"Would you play a song before I go back?" asked Haana. Skeetu took out the flute and made it sing. The sahaar got to her feet and swayed around the fire.

"What are you doing? Did you eat a bad mudbug?"

"No," said Haana. "It is dancing. Come. Try it." The oldkin stood and started moving as her friend did.

"You need the flute song, Skeetu. Make the song and move where it pulls you." Skeetu played and the two danced around the flames.

Chapter 15

A moon cycle later, Haana returned with her friends. Soohla, was the tallest of the three. Her raven-colored hair was wrapped with a thin strip of hide and held in place high over her head, making her seem taller yet. When Skeetu first saw her face up close, she jumped back. The sahaar had eyes the color of a cold winter sky. She laughed at the oldkin's startled reaction. Dami's eyes were like Haana's, brown as the nut of the fingerleaf tree. She was the same size as herself, with a nose nearly as large. Her skin was lighter than that of Haana and Soohla's, but still a bit darker than hers. When the sun hit her hair at certain angles, Skeetu saw a faint hint of orange fire in the black. *We are all different,* thought Skeetu, *even the ones who are the same.* The days were still warm and none of them wore the mammoth skins of winter. Instead, they, along with Skeetu, dressed in lighter elk hides. The oldkin looked at the carved shell hanging against Dami's chest. It was held in place by twisted grasses looped around her neck.

"Do you carry food for a later meal?" she asked in oldkin, forgetting the sahaar would not understand her. When Skeetu and Haana spoke, they mostly used oldkin words, as Haana was faster at learning them than Skeetu was at learning sahaar. The oldkin could mimic any bird in the forest, but while she could understand the sahaar words, she had difficulty pronouncing them.

Dami furrowed her brow and looked to Haana. Haana smiled and answered for her.

"It is not food," she said to Skeetu, in the oldkin's language. "It is a… way to make good things happen."

"But it is just a scratched shell."

"Dami made the scratches. That makes it more than a shell," said Haana. She repeated what she said to the two sahaar. Skeetu understood most of it. Dami said something back to her.

"Dami says it is also pretty," said her friend.

"Haana?" asked Skeetu.

"What?"

"I know," said Skeetu. She pointed to Dami. "I do understand your sahaar words. I just need get better at speaking to them."

Haana laughed. "I forgot."

"Ay sahaar? Na ti sahaar," said Dami, pointing to Skeetu.

Haana laughed again. "She said that she's not sah—stranger, you are stranger…"

"I understood that," said the oldkin. "But the word still confuses me."

Bulo came crashing through the undergrowth and stopped at the girls. He stared at the two newcomers. Soohla and Dami stood to run. Haana motioned for them to wait. She got up and walked to the rhino and stroked its head. She told them Bulo would not harm them. The girls spoke with Haana, in a panicked tone, too fast for Skeetu to understand.

"They say it is hard to finally see the… beast of stories they have heard," said Haana. "Like me, they heard tales of you and Bulo, the great spearnose. Tales of fright and… caution."

"We are just an oldkin and a spearnose," said Skeetu. "We are no more than that." Then she looked up at the towering woolly rhino. "*I* am no more than that," she added. "He maybe is."

Over the next few months, the four gathered frequently in Skeetu's woods. At first, the forest was a frightening place for her friends. They did not like feeling closed in by thick trees. Anything could be out there, watching them, unseen. Like the wolf. Even when they did not see it, they felt it in the shadows. Having Bulo nearby was some comfort, although they learned to be ready to dart when he went into his fits of wildness. In time, Haana and Soohla grew to think of the forest as a second home and came to embrace this shelter from the chilling winds. Dami, less so. Skeetu suspected that she was often along only to be with the other two.

Skeetu was happy she was no longer alone. She had Bulo, but Bulo was not one like herself. These sahaar were like herself. She found that every day they looked less and less odd to her, to the point where they did not look odd at all. Their shapes were a little different, but inside they were the same. The oldkin had grown better at speaking their language, and they were quickly learning hers. Soon it was as easy to talk with the two girls as it was with Haana.

Soohla was the funny one. She moved as a long-legged bird and could make many animal sounds, much like Skeetu. She did things wrong on purpose, to make them laugh. Sometimes she would fall from a tree. Or slip on a wet molefruit skin. At first, Skeetu wasn't sure if she should laugh at the girl lying splayed on the ground. But Soohla would stay down until someone did. Then she'd pop up with a big grin on her face, often marred by a bloody nose or new bruise.

Dami said little. She always appeared lost in her own self. She rarely smiled and the oldkin wondered why she joined her friends, since she did not seem to enjoy their company, either. What she did seem to enjoy was complaining about things.

"Bulo smells bad," she said.

"I know," said Skeetu. "Many things smell bad."

"Many things don't choose to lay next to us."

"Then move him," said the oldkin.

Soohla laughed. "I will do it." She stood and walked over to Bulo and pushed against him as hard as she could. The rhino lifted his head and looked at her, lazily. "I need help!" Haana and Skeetu joined her, and the three threw themselves against the beast, who seemed uninterested in moving, and therefore did not.

"Come on, Dami! Maybe one more!" shouted Soohla. Bulo belched. The three exploded in laughter and fell to the ground, against the foul-smelling spearnose. Skeetu laughed hardest of all. Then it occurred to her. *We laugh as one! We laugh as one!* It was as good as she thought it would be.

"It is not funny," said Dami. "Now you all stink." This, of course, made them laugh even harder.

A few days later, Haana and Soohla hunted with Skeetu along the river. The sahaar girls had promised their mothers they would bring back fish for their families. Skeetu knew of many pockets where they gathered and could easily be speared.

"I am sorry Dami is angry with me," said the oldkin. She thrust her spear into the churning water and pulled out a wriggling fish. She struck it on a rock to stop it from fighting and dropped it into Soohla's sack.

"How did you know this?" asked Haana.

"You told me this morning," said Skeetu.

"Oh. I forgot. I think she is angry with me, too," said Haana. "And Soohla. She did not like us laughing at her."

"In front of you," added Soohla.

"Aren't you afraid she will tell the sahaar that you come here?" asked Skeetu.

"I don't think she would," said Haana.

"She won't," said Soohla. "She knows it would anger Rin."

"She doesn't want to anger Rin. Why not?" asked the oldkin. Soohla looked at Haana uncomfortably and shrugged her shoulders.

"She was not always with our clan," said Soohla. "Her father showed up with her when she was a baby. He would not talk about her mother."

"Where did she come from?" asked Skeetu.

"He would not talk about that, either. He still does not. Of course, Dami remembers nothing."

"What will happen if she does tell your sahaar about our… friendship?" asked Skeetu.

"I do not know about Haana," said Soohla, "But Father will keep me in the valley. And they might send out hunters to… find you. Oldkin are bad luck! Just to see you will… make our eyes fall out!"

Haana laughed. "Why do you do this to us, Skeetu? Why do you blind your *sahaar* friends?"

Soohla closed her eyes and stumbled along the riverbank. "It has happened already! Curses to you, oldkin! My eyes are gone!"

Skeetu gave her a playful shove and the girl splashed into the cold water. The oldkin sometimes forgot how strong she was. Soohla dropped her sack and the fish fell out.

"The fish!" shouted Haana. They were being carried downstream. Skeetu jumped in the water and gathered up as many as she could. Soohla managed to grab a couple, too.

"I am sorry," said the oldkin, shivering in her wet hides. Soohla was just as wet but didn't seem to mind.

"It is that bad luck," she said, smiling. "See? They are right about you!"

They went back to the camp and Skeetu woke the fire outside her shelter to dry her skins. Bulo was out roaming somewhere. She wasn't worried. He often took off on his own to do whatever spearnoses did when they were not with her. She looked up and scanned the rocky hillside for the wolf but did not see it. That was not unusual, either. Haana dropped three of the smaller fish onto the coals to cook them. Their scales were smooth and would not need to be scraped off. The smell made Skeetu's mouth water. She searched the area again, wondering where Bulo had gone. Then she saw something, far in the distance.

"Who is that?" she asked. The other two stood and looked where she pointed.

"Who is what?" asked Haana. Neither could see what the oldkin's sharp eyes could pick out.

"Someone is coming," said Skeetu. "Rin?"

Haana's brother ran toward them. When he reached the girls, he slowed, looking for Bulo.

"He's not here," said Skeetu, in sahaar. Rin looked around, not quite trusting her.

"He's not here," said Haana. "He will not hurt you anyway." But the young sahaar man looked worried. He walked briskly up to his sister, waving his hands frantically.

"What's wrong?" asked Soohla.

"Something in the valley," said Haana. "Mother?" Rin grabbed Haana's arm and pulled her as he ran.

"Come, Soohla," shouted the girl. "Something is bad. We have to go!"

The three sahaar raced from the forest. Skeetu stood and watched as they disappeared in the distance. *Cave bear? What else could bring them such fear? Clawtooth?* Bulo trotted back into the camp. He settled in next to the fire, more because the oldkin was there than for the warmth. The wolf howled in the distance.

Chapter 16

The moon filled and emptied since Skeetu's friends left with Rin. She was tempted to go to the sahaar camp to see if she could learn what happened. But she did not. It would no longer feel right to watch them in secret, now that they were her friends.

One morning, she crawled out of her shelter to find a figure sitting by the fire. The flames were roaring, built up to chase away the cold bite of dawn.

"Soohla!"

"Skeetu. You sleep late."

"Where have you been? Where is Haana? Why did you not wake me?" Bulo, who slept next to the shelter, climbed to his feet. He had seen the sahaar arrive earlier, but knew her, and had gone back to sleep. He shook the coat of snow from his hide and lumbered off to the forest edge to fill his belly.

"I was thinking of what I was going to say. Haana cannot leave," said Soohla. "They know about you. They say you bring us sickness."

"How do they know she was with me?" asked Skeetu.

"They asked. Haana could not lie when asked by her father. Nearly all are sick now. Most have fallen to the deep valley. More fall with each roll of the sun."

The oldkin didn't know what to say. "Is… is Haana sick, too?"

"No. I am not, either. Or Dami. Or Rin."

"What kind of sick? I can find you herbs that may help."

"We have herbs, too. Nothing helps. It is very bad, Skeetu! I am frightened for my friends! My baby brothers are gone. My family… gone. I am frightened for *me* but feel I should not say it! I should be brave. But I see the sickness. The skin grows bumps, and bleeds. What is inside us, comes out as black water from all holes. We become weak as worms. And then…" Soohla stared into the fire. Skeetu had never seen her like this before. She was always on the edge of saying or doing something to make them all laugh. She wished she would now, to chase away the dread she felt.

"Are you afraid of me? Of a sickness I bring?" asked the oldkin, after a brief silence. Soohla looked up at her. Skeetu was transfixed by her clear, blue eyes. She always was. *Do they see like my eyes?* Then the sahaar smiled.

"No, Skeetu. I did wonder to myself if you brought us this sickness. But then I thought, 'Haana was with Skeetu, and is not sick. Dami was with Skeetu and is not sick. Rin was with Skeetu and is not sick. And Soohla was with Skeetu and is not sick.' The sickness comes from another place. Those who are not sick were with *you*. I came here to bring you back with me."

Skeetu was about to throw a stick onto the fire and stopped. "Go back with you?" She stood and looked down at the sahaar. "I do not think that would be wise."

"Skeetu. We are not sick because you *chase it away*! You can chase it from my home!"

The oldkin stood, unmoving, trying to imagine herself walking into their valley. A place where she was feared. They would fill her with spears before she reached their fires. *But what if I can chase their sickness from them? How? Is it something I must do, or say? Is it enough for me to just be among them?*

"Do you know I can do this? I can chase a fox and a hare, but I would not know how to chase a... sickness."

"But somehow you did! Will you try? Will you come with me?"

"Yes. I will not bring Bulo, though."

"No! No, you should not!"

They set out for the valley. Skeetu thought she should leave her spear behind but changed her mind. She had seen the tracks of a clawtooth a few days ago.

"Why won't they attack me when they see me?" she asked her friend.

"I will be with you. And Rin. There he is up ahead. He agrees with me, that you might help us, but he still does not trust you."

"Or Bulo."

"Or Bulo."

They caught up with the sahaar. "Hello, Rin," said Skeetu. She didn't care that Rin did not want to go near her. She liked him anyway, because of how he looked out for his sister. Only once did she see him smile, and it was from a great distance. Still, it was a sight that brought her a surprising rush of joy.

Rin's and her eyes met for an instant. Then he quickly turned away and walked briskly toward his home. Skeetu could keep up easily, but Soohla kept falling back.

"Rin," said the oldkin. "Can we go slower? I can't walk into your valley without her to speak for me." He looked back and shot her a warning look, and then picked up his pace. They had reached the end of the riverbank and were about to embark along the canyon ridge when Rin stopped short. Skeetu, and then Soohla, caught up and stood beside him. The young man pointed to something in the distance.

"What is it?" asked Soohla. "I don't see anything."

"It is Haana," said Skeetu. "And Dami. And someone… old."

"How do you know?" asked the girl. Rin had turned to look at her, too.

"I can see them. You cannot?"

"No," said Soohla. "Do the oldkin have owl eyes in their head?"

The others made their way along the lip of the canyon, while the three from the forest rushed to meet up with them. Skeetu saw fear on their faces. They were running from something.

"Turn around," said Haana when they reached one another. She was out of breath. Her cheeks were stained with the salt of tears. Rin rushed up to her. Skeetu watched his hands moving frantically. She wished she understood him, as his sister did, but she was fairly sure she knew what he was asking.

The old man stepped forward. "This is the creature who walks with the spearnose? This is what we feared?" Skeetu expected him to laugh, but instead he bent forward to study her face more closely. "I do not fear you," he said. "This I know. And now this *you* know."

"Good?" said Skeetu, taking a step back. He moved forward but Rin got between them. He shook his head 'no' and the man backed up. Skeetu looked up at the boy, confused. *Did he just protect me?* Dami stepped up beside Haana's brother and glowered at the oldkin, as if she had done something wrong. Her eyes, too, were red from tears.

"What happened?" asked Soohla.

"They are gone," said Haana.

"Gone? Where? Have we moved?"

"Gone, to the deep valley."

"Everyone? I only left in the night. In one night, they all… died?"

"We are all that are left," said Haana. "The sickness came like a snakecat. It bit everyone, one after another and another, and then came back in the morning to take away its weakened meals. One, after another and another… There are only the rats left. More now than ever. The sickness does not take them.”

“So… where do we go? What do we do?” asked Soohla.

“I don’t know,” said Haana. “We just had to get away. We did not know if we would be next to fall. A thing came to live in our valley that we cannot see, or fight. So we run so it cannot catch us.”

“Skeetu was our chance to fight this thing. We did not get the sickness because she was with each of us. But we waited too long,” said Soohla.

“What about Chup?” asked Dami, pointing to the old man. “He was never near Skeetu, and he is not sick.”

“Will this animal make us all sick in the end?” asked Chup. “I have seen their kind before, and now I see them no longer. They are falling dead everywhere, and maybe what drops them is what pushed our clan into the deep valley. This I do not know.”

“I am not an animal,” said Skeetu. “And I do not make anyone sick.”

“This I do not know,” Chup repeated.

“This I do know,” said the oldkin. She did not like him talking about her family, ‘falling dead everywhere’. What killed them was a cave bear, not a valley sickness. She felt no need to tell him this, though.

“So what do we do?” repeated Soohla.

“There is a clan beyond the scrubhills,” said Chup. “We go to them.”

"That is very far," said Dami. "And it is getting colder."

"There are no clans closer. This I know."

"Do you mean the hills beyond the forest?" asked Skeetu.

"Yes," said Haana.

"I know of those hills. It will take you a long time to reach them. More now with the cold and snow coming. You can stay by my fire tonight. Bulo and I have chased off the wolves, most of them."

"That might be a good place to start from," said Haana. Her brother turned to her and frowned.

"Oh stop," scolded his sister. "He won't hurt you."

"Who?" asked Chup.

"Bulo," said Haana.

"Skeetu's friend. Spearnose," added Soohla.

"That tale is true?" asked Chup. "I thought it was just stories made bigger with words."

"You will see he is bigger than the stories," said Soohla.

Dami reached up and rested her hand on Rin's shoulder. She patted the shell that hung on her chest. "This will keep us safe." Rin frowned. He pointed to her shell and then back toward their valley.

"That could not be stopped," said Dami, simply.

It was dark when they reached Skeetu's camp. She built up the fire to warm the group and shared one of the hares she had caught the day before.

"Your kind can make fire? That I did not know," said Chup. His teeth tore out a string of meat from the hare's leg bone. Skeetu noticed his fingers. They were like knobby, twisted branches. His meal was mostly held, with difficulty, between his palms.

"She cannot," said Dami. "They don't know how to, the old kind."

"Yes, I can!" said Skeetu. "Haana showed me!"

"They don't know how to *on their own*," corrected Dami. "We have to show them how to do things."

The oldkin got up and walked away.

"Where do you go?" asked Soohla.

"I am getting featherleaf branches for you to sleep on," said Skeetu. She turned to Dami. "You can find your own. Do I need to show you how?"

Dami sniffed and said nothing. Haana stood and joined the oldkin. She helped her pull down some branches and snap them off the tree. Rin did the same. He was taller than them and could reach higher to get more of the branch. Skeetu felt him looking at her. He always had a mildly confused expression on his face when he watched her. When she looked back at him, he turned his face away. *I am just a curious animal to the sahaar. A spirit. A sickness. One who could not start fires with rocks and has to be shown.* She stole a longer glance at the young sahaar man. *He is curious to me, too, I suppose.*

Bulo dozed by her shelter. He showed little interest in the new sahaar who joined them that evening.

"That one does not have killing eyes," Chup conceded. "This I know. Are all spearnoses like this one?"

"This is the only one I know," said Skeetu.

"Do all your old kind live among beasts?"

"I don't know."

***

The sun had set. The six sat around the fire, saying very little. *The sahaar have lost everything,* thought Skeetu. *It will never leave their thoughts.* She pulled the flute out from her boot.

"Play a song for those fallen in the deep valley," said Haana.

"You made a flute?" asked Chup.

"She cannot," said Dami. "Even when Haana shows her."

"She can play it better than I can," said Haana.

"And you, Dami" added Soohla.

Skeetu thought about their loss. She did not know the sahaar who… fell to the deep valley. But she did remember that first night alone after losing her family. She brought the flute to her lips and played what she felt like inside. At one point, she looked up at Chup, who was weeping. Skeetu stopped.

"I am sorry," she said.

"No," said Chup, wiping his tears with the back of his hand. "Keep playing."

113

Chapter 17

"Where is Rin?" asked Haana. The group was awake and milling about, worn down from a night of thoughts racing through dark unknowns. Skeetu had stayed in her shelter and offered to share it with Haana and Soohla. *Not Dami. She can sleep on the cold dirt.* They chose instead to be together, sahaar with the sahaar. The oldkin understood. Sometimes she felt like she was one of them, but then she'd be reminded she was not.

"I don't know," said Soohla.

"This is not a time to be wandering off alone," said Chup. "We need to stay together if we are to make it to the scrubhills. This I do know!"

"I will find him," said Skeetu. She knew the land well. The oldkin sprinted across the clearing and disappeared into the trees.

"You trust her?" Chup asked Haana, once the oldkin was gone.

"I trust her," said the girl.

"She is not *us*."

"Yes, she is," said the girl.

Skeetu ran through the woods. She did not tell the others, but she was worried that Rin would find the clawtooth. Or that it would find him. He would not be able to call out if he did. She had once asked Haana why he could not speak. Her friend shrugged and said it was just always so. She heard a pounding behind her and turned to see Bulo racing to catch up. *Good*, she thought. The ground was now covered in powdery snow, so the sahaar's tracks would be easy to find. In the time she lived here, she had found that when she set out with no plan of where she was going, the sloping land usually led her to the same place, to a shallow depression in the lower hills. Skeetu headed in that direction. Then she spotted his footprints.

"Rin!" she called out. The tracks did not lead down, but up, to an outcropping that stood free of the trees. She knew that spot and had returned to it many times with the flute she received from Haana. The oldkin and her spearnose walked up a gravelly path and came upon the young man. He stood on the ledge, looking into the distance.

"Rin!" said Skeetu. He turned and looked at the oldkin, unsurprised to see her. Then he saw Bulo and flinched.

"What are you doing?" asked Skeetu. Rin pointed to the hills in the distance.

"The scrubhills. It's where you are going." The sahaar nodded. Then he waved his hand back and forth at the landscape.

"You do not want to go?" Rin shook his head. He made stabbing motions with his hands, as if spears pierced his chest.

"They will kill you. The new sahaar will kill you? You are afraid?" The sahaar touched his chest and again shook his head. Then he held out his hand, hovering at the height of his sister, and nodded.

"You are afraid for Haana," guessed Skeetu. "Why does Chup want to go there?" Rin tried to answer her but could not make himself understood. He threw his hands down in frustration and brushed past the oldkin as he marched back to the camp. *I am always making him angry*, she thought. When Skeetu and Bulo caught up, he was arguing with Haana, his hands ablur. Dami stood beside him, as she often did, nodding in agreement with what he was trying to communicate. This went on for some time and the oldkin went into her shelter. She did not want to be with the others right now. There were going to be problems. *Who is their leader now? Bent-fingered Chup? Who is Chup?* She chipped away at the edges of her blackstone spearhead. It had struck a rock while hunting hole-rats and needed a new tip. After a while, Haana joined her.

"We are going," she said.

"Who?"

"All."

"Rin, too?" asked Skeetu. "He did not want to. He said it is dangerous."

"I know. He is worried about me. I am all he has left, he said. I told him I will keep myself safe. He still does not believe me, but that changes nothing."

"Is Chup Leader now?" asked Skeetu.

"I think so," said Haana. "He was not before. Before everything… But he has watched the moon fill and empty more times than any of us. He has seen more of this land than any of us. He has seen the sahaar we travel to. And he has the age to prove he knows how to stay alive. We follow those who have lived through the most. It has always been our way."

"That is good, then"

"Maybe," said the girl. "But it is he who says we may not be welcomed. They chased him off with spears when he found them, but that was a very long time ago. He was just a boy."

"They could be gone."

"Most of those who chased him will be. And maybe their children are different. Maybe they will greet us with wide smiles and warm hides."

"I do not think you should go," said Skeetu. "Why would you? And it is not an easy place to get to."

"We need others to live. We are not like… *you*, Skeetu."

"But they will chase you off!"

"Maybe. But what are we to do? We cannot return to our valley. It was swallowed by the sickness from the valley below."

"You could stay here with me. Oldkin need others, too, Haana."

"Chup would not want that. He wants to find our people."

"What about *you*, Haana? *You* could stay with me."

"Or you could come with us," said the sahaar.

Skeetu thought about that, not that she hadn't already. It might not be bad, living with the sahaar. But what about the sahaar in the scrubhills? They did not even welcome their own kind.

Soohla crawled into the shelter.

"Is she coming with us?" she asked Haana.

"I don't know," said her friend.

"I do not think the scrubhills' sahaar, or Chup, would welcome me," said Skeetu.

"That is okay," said Soohla. "We will probably never find them. Chup said it was long ago since he had been there. He was just a boy, lost, trying to find his way home. He remembers the place, but not how he got there."

"I know how to get there," said Skeetu. "It looks close from here, but it is a trip with many twists and drops. I have done it, but I did not see any sahaar. I did not go past the foothills, though."

"Why did you go there?" asked Haana.

Skeetu smiled. "I followed Bulo. I sometimes go where he goes. He has taken me for journeys that have lasted many days and many nights. I have no one else to be with, so I follow him. We walk. We eat. We sleep. It does not matter where. We once went to the foot of the scrubhills. There are plants there he likes. I have wondered if it is where he had come from with his mother."

"Well, that is it, then, oldkin. You are coming with us. We need you," said Soohla.

"You know the way to go," added Haana.

"Talk to Chup," said Skeetu. "He will not want me."

They left the shelter and found the old man. He was busy re-stringing the stone point to his spear. Most of the work was done with his teeth, which he had grown adept at using in place of his fingers.

"Skeetu is coming with us," announced Soohla. Chup looked up at the oldkin and said nothing.

"Do you think she should?" asked Dami. "They will see her long arms and big feet and know she is not us."

"They will see your little pebble eyes and hear your bitter tongue and know you are not us, either," said Soohla. She looked up at Chup, waiting for him to say something.

"After what you just said to Dami, I will not risk saying the wrong thing. That I do know," he said.

"She knows the way," said Haana. "She's been to the foot of the scrubhills."

"That would a good reason for her to come," said the old man. He looked past Skeetu to where Bulo was rubbing his rump against a tree. "Would that one be joining us?"

"He would have to," said Skeetu. "He's the one we would be following."

Rin stood and walked away from the group. Skeetu could see pain in his face. She wondered if his misgivings about this plan were about more than his concern for his sister's safety. He got just a few steps away and then turned around. He strode up to Chup; their faces were just a breath apart. The young man pointed at the old one and then spread his arms wide. He gestured toward the girls and then slapped his chest. Chup squinted as he tried to read what the boy was saying. He looked over to his sister.

"He wants to know why you are now Leader," said Haana.

"I am not Leader," said Chup. "And if I was, I would take no pride in leading a clan of children. If you do not wish to go to the scrubhills, then you do not have to. I will find my way there alone. This I do know!"

Rin made some more motions with his hands. Skeetu knew what he was saying.

"Why do you not want to go?" asked Dami. He seemed to be the only one she spoke kindly to.

"He told me on the ledge. He does not trust them. He said he thinks the other sahaar will attack them," said Skeetu.

"They might," agreed Chup. "But sahaar need sahaar. It is the strength of the clan that keeps us alive." Rin gestured back toward their valley, where the strength of a clan did them no good.

"Rin is saying 'what about them?'" said Haana. "But I do not agree with him. We do need others. I will go with Chup. Rin, you are coming, too. You will see it is the thing to do."

"Which means Dami is going," mumbled Soohla.

"What?" asked Dami.

"Nothing."

The others agreed, as did Rin, though he was visibly unhappy with the decision.

"Are we ready?" asked Chup, as he heaved his pouch onto his shoulder.

Skeetu quickly gathered her things, few that they were. Living alone was not something she chose. And not how she wished to live. She had realized that all the more when she finally found friends. The time spent apart from them always felt too long. If they left her, that time apart would be endless. She walked up to Bulo, whispered something in his ear and gave him a slap. The wooly rhino turned and pushed through the trees behind them.

"We follow him," said the oldkin.

Chup turned back toward Rin. "Do you see? I am not Leader. Leader is a spearnose!"

Chapter 18

The group had been traveling for two days. Bulo went at his own pace, which was sometimes hard to keep up with, and other times frustratingly slow. He hadn't slipped into any of his wild fits, which was good, since they were often moving through tight spaces that left little room for escape. Night began to set in, and Rin built a fire against a large boulder. He had taken down a young elk along the way, which he and Dami butchered and wrapped in its own hide. No one spoke much, the sting of the loss of their clan still very fresh. Skeetu could feel their sadness as if it were a thing she could reach out and touch. Mothers, fathers, sisters, brothers, aunts and uncles… children, all gone in so short a time. *How did this happen? Will it happen again?*

The heat from the flames bounced off the rock, warming them. They ate in silence, each in their own thoughts, and Skeetu took out her flute. It did not feel like a time to play it, but she found it comforting to hold in her fingers.

"How does one of the old kind, make such sounds?" asked Chup. "You are not known for such things, but you play like no other I have heard."

"I use the songs of the birds," said Skeetu. She whistled the notes of a honeylark and then played them on the instrument. "Then I join them with sounds I hear in my own head."

"I wonder what you could do with a *whisperflute*," said the old man.

"What is that?" asked Haana.

"It is known that a flute made with a leg of the stickleg bird can speak to those who have gone to the deep valley. It is a special bird that few have seen. I have, but only once. It has a long beak, a longer neck, and even longer legs made from the branches of a puff willow. The one I found had a blood red patch on its head." He looked at Skeetu. "Redder than what grows from your head. I saw it, and then I did not see it. It flew off before I could get near."

"I have never seen one," said Skeetu. "If I do, I will spear it and make a whisperflute."

"You cannot make flutes," said Dami.

Skeetu glared at her. "Why do you always speak of things I cannot do?"

Dami shrugged.

"No," said Chup. "You must not kill the sticklegs! This I do know! But you must be with it as it dies, to join what is inside you with what is inside the bird. When the bone is carved, and the holes are drilled, the flute's song seeks the sticklegs in the deep valley, and the sahaar who have fallen there."

Rin looked at the man suspiciously. He shook his head 'no'.

"You do not believe me, boy. I see that. But you still have much to learn. We live on because we learn to trust the words of others. The words of those who have lived the span of your life many times over. This I know!"

"I believe you," said Soohla. "My uncle spoke of this. He called it a *windflute,* but his words were as yours. The sticklegs live in turtle bogs, he said, but he has never seen one."

"Your uncle's father was Bindin, and I have heard with my ears his telling of the special bird. It is where your uncle learned of them," said Chup. "We two are the only from our clan to have seen it." Rin gestured like he was holding a flute and then held out his palms.

"He wants to know how you—" began Haana.

"I know. I know," said Chup. "He says, 'How do you know. It is how I know of anything that happened when I was not there to see it. We learn from sahaar who *were* there. And if they were *not* there, they have learned it from another who was. And if that another was not there, it was learned from another yet. Stories travel. Some listen. Some do not. I do. This you should know."

Skeetu pictured playing her flute for the oldkin who joined the lights in the sky. She wondered if it would work for her, or if it only reached the sahaar in the deep valley. She always imagined her family listening to her when she played. With the whisperflute, she could let them know she was okay. And that she thought of them every day and every night. The thought of it filled her chest with warm clouds. What a gift she could give!

"I will find this bird someday," she said.

"I will help," said Haana. Rin mimed the spears hitting his chest again. His sister added, "He said if the sahaar we seek do not first send us to the deep valley."

"He is right," said Dami, looking up at the boy.

"Then why are you with us?" asked Soohla.

"Where else would I go?"

"You could have stayed behind."

"No, she couldn't," said Haana. "She is with us. She is our sister."

***

They traveled five more days. At one point, Bulo slipped into his madness and galloped around the group, running down invisible foes. Rin was nearly trampled but managed to shimmy up a tree just in time. He watched from above, appearing somewhat amused by the encounter. Chup and Dami leapt onto a rock, out of reach. Soohla, Haana, and Skeetu froze where they were. They were used to this and knew that none of them would be singled out for attack. The spearnose was fully unaware of them and would charge and thrust at the air as he ran around them. It was over as quickly as it began. The rhino looked at Skeetu and then continued on his way. Rin moved from the front of the group to the rear, as far from Bulo as he could get.

"How much further?" asked Dami.

"Another few days if the snow holds up," said Skeetu. The sky had been growing a deeper gray. A snowstorm would surely slow them down.

"What if Bulo decides he has gone far enough?" asked Chup.

"He might," said the oldkin. "I think then we would have to go on our own—you, at least. Or turn back."

"We can't turn back now," said Haana.

"We won't," said Soohla.

"No, we won't," agreed Chup. "Even if we don't find the sahaar where I saw them, we may still find them in other places. Or a different clan." He looked down at Dami. "Maybe we will find *your* sahaar." Dami frowned and shook her head. She dropped back to walk with Rin.

The six and the woolly rhino reached a high ledge. They could see the scrubhills in the distance, closer, but still days away.

"We should stop here for the night," said Chup. "We don't want to be climbing down there in the dark."

"Can Bulo go down that ridge? It looks steep," said Soohla.

Skeetu smiled. "Yes. He knows a way. But Chup is right. We should not do it in the dark."

"Does any of this look familiar to you?" asked Haana.

"This place, no," answered Chup. "The scrubhills, yes, but I went to them a different way."

"I think I remember a cave along here," said Skeetu. "I was afraid to go in it alone, though."

"If there is one, do you really think it would be empty?" asked Dami.

"Probably not," said Haana.

Skeetu shot a look at Dami. "That's why I didn't go in."

It began to snow. "It might be worth having a look," said Chup. "Maybe it will be empty."

They searched the rock wall for a way inside. The snow was sticky wet and falling fast. It was soon up to their knees. Bulo walked ahead of them, carving a path. They heard a whistle behind them.

"It's Rin," said Skeetu. "Maybe he found it."

The group rushed back to the young man, who pointed to an opening through a break in the wall. Rin cautiously peered inside.

"Do you see anything?" asked Dami. He shook his head. Then he went inside. The group outside heard him take a sharp breath. Skeetu rushed in, spear ready for a fight. Then she stopped, and let out a gasp, as well.

"What is this?" she asked. Rin looked at her and smiled. He motioned rubbing something on the wall. A herd of goats was rendered on the stone. The others came inside.

"Hornbeards!" said Soohla. "Who drew this?"

"Maybe the sahaar we seek?" suggested Chup. "This must be a hunting shelter. The drawings give them power for a good hunt."

"They made this. But how?" asked Skeetu.

Rin picked up a piece of charcoal from the floor. He rubbed an image of a goat on the wall. Then he looked at Skeetu and held out his hand as if to say, 'Like this'.

"You have never seen a picture before?" asked Dami.

"No."

"Maybe that is why there are none of you left," said the girl. "You do not know how to make the power for the hunt."

Skeetu was annoyed with those words, at first. But where *did* all the oldkin go? *Maybe she is right.*

"I do not like this," said Chup, pointing to the ground at a pile of cave hyena droppings. There were several, and they were fresh.

"Batbears," said Skeetu.

They looked outside the cave. The snow was falling hard.

"I think we have no choice," said Chup. "We either get buried in snow, or we fight batbears when they come back. This I do know."

"We don't know that they will return tonight," said Soohla. "But we do know we do not want to be outside."

Rin pushed a pile outside with the bone of a shoulder blade left from a meal, probably from a young cave bear. He walked to the back sat against the wall. The others settled in as well. There was no wood for a fire, so they'd have to huddle for warmth. Not something Skeetu was used to, having lived alone for so long. Bulo had disappeared, but Skeetu was not worried. He was probably rooting in the snow for food somewhere. He would never wander too far from her.

The sun went down, leaving them in near total darkness. Once their eyes adjusted, they could see only the dark outlines of one another. Skeetu's eyes were stronger than those of the sahaar, and she could make out their faces. None of them looked happy to be here.

"Wish we had a fire," said Dami.

"Me, too," said Haana.

"Too bad bones don't burn," added Soohla. "They're everywhere."

"Do you hear that?" asked Skeetu. They stopped talking and listened. A string of low moans broke through the muffled silence of the snowfall. They were distant but growing closer.

"Batbears," said Chup. "I am guessing they *are* coming back. Grab your spears. They travel together. There could be more of them than there are of us."

The calls grew louder, and more frenzied. The batbears were now yipping and screaming. The hairs on the back of Skeetu's neck prickled against her cloak.

"They know we are here," she said.

One stepped up to the entrance. It was joined by another. And then a third one, each larger than two sahaar combined. All the group could see of them were their broad, shadowy forms, darker than the night sky. Their breaths were rapid and smelled of the foulness of the rotten meat they ate. Rin leapt up and ran at them, thrusting his spear at the beasts. They deftly avoided each jab and snapped at him with their powerful jaws, flowing back to him with each retreat. There was a yip and a whine. *He got one,* thought Skeetu.

"My spear! I dropped it! I can't find it!" shouted Chup. Skeetu knew his fingers were weak and bent with age. He could no longer hold the rocks to start fires, or pull the pelt off a hare. What could he do with a spear?

Still, she said, "Here, take mine." She pushed the shaft of her spear into the old man's hands and turned toward the commotion. The oldkin screamed and jumped on the back of one of the batbears. She wrapped her powerful arms around its neck and squeezed. She could barely reach her wrist to grab tight with her other hand. The third one came at her, but Rin pricked it with his spear. It turned on him quickly, too fast for the sahaar to recoil and strike again.

"*No!*" yelled Dami, rushing out from behind the young man. She thrust her spear into the beast's chest, and it fell to the ground, dead.

"*Help!*" called Skeetu, still holding on to the batbear. It spun in circles, snapping its jaw as it tried to turn and grab the girl.

"Skeetu, let go!" shouted Soohla. "I'll get it!" The oldkin rolled off the animal and landed on Chup's missing spear. She picked it up but didn't need it. Rin and Soohla came at the batbear from two directions and pierced it from both sides. Haana ran to the entrance of the cave. She held the point of her spear out in front of her.

"There are more of them out there," she said.

"Why aren't they coming in?" asked Soohla.

"They are waiting for us," said Chup.

It was a little brighter outside, the white snow still holding what little light there was in the night sky. It was coming down heavy, though, hiding what lurked in the distance. Skeetu's arms were numb, spent from trying to squeeze the life from a batbear's neck. *Please stay out there. Please stay out there.*

Suddenly, from the wall of white, there came a muffled bellow.

"Bulo!" shouted Skeetu. She pushed into the snow. The woolly rhino called out again. "I'm coming!" answered the oldkin. Its call was joined by the high-pitched squeals of the batbears. *"I'm coming!"* Bulo could run down one or two of these animals, but if they were able to surround him, he would be ripped apart. She saw him in the distance. He was holding his ground, charging and retreating as they came at him from all directions. One of them saw her and turned away from the attack on the spearnose. Bulo skewered it with his horn. Skeetu felt something grab her shoulder. She turned, ready to fight, but it was Rin. He motioned for them to split up. The oldkin heard a yelp as a spear flew past her and landed in one of the beasts.

"Got it!" said Soohla. Another spear flew and took out another. Rin ran forward and was about to throw his spear when he slipped in the snow. One of the batbears saw this and rushed toward him. It was three leaps away, having to clear the height of the deepening snow. Rin held up his hands, ready for it to land on him. The spearnose was right behind it. It plowed straight through, taking it out just before it reached the sahaar.

The remaining batbears—no one was really sure how many there were—ran off. What was to be an easy feast left them beaten and fewer in number. Skeetu went up to the spearnose, who had collapsed in the snow. He was bleeding from multiple bites.

"I am sorry, my friend," she said. Rin joined her, for the first time showing no fear of the animal. He reached out and stroked Bulo's nose. The young man looked at Skeetu, his eyes showing deep concern for the beast that had saved him. The rest of the sahaar walked up to the three of them.

"Will he be all right?" asked Haana.

"I don't know," said Skeetu.

"What should we do?" asked Chup. "He is our guide."

"He is my friend!" snapped the oldkin. "I don't care about your sahaar in the scrubhills!"

"I mean… I know," said the old man.

"We can't bring him in with us. And if he stays here, they might come back for him," said Soohla.

"I am staying with him," said Skeetu.

"In this storm?" asked Dami.

"I am staying with him," the oldkin repeated. She dropped down on the ground and leaned against her spearnose for warmth. *Do not grow cold on me like your mother.* Haana said nothing but sat down beside her friend. Soohla did the same. Rin walked around to the other side of the rhino and slid down into the snow, his back against Bulo. Chup and Dami looked at one another and then joined the rest of their group.

Only Bulo slept that night.

Far in the distance, so far that Skeetu wasn't certain she heard it, a wolf howled.

Chapter 19

The forty-eight hours were up. Jennifer Moore raced through the desert in her rented Jeep, hoping to reach the Neandergirl's resting place before dark. Dugg sat in the passenger seat, slobbering up the window. She worried about bringing him to the desert, but knew that with some extra precautions, German Shepherds did okay in the heat. With so much whirling through her head, she hadn't slept in two days. She had managed to get through customs with the flute. Despite what had happened to her on the last trip, she chose not to mention having it in her luggage. If she got caught, she—well, she didn't know what she'd do, but she was taking this as far as she could. The archeologist reasoned it would be less risky to bring it into Spain than into the United States. If she was discovered, at least she was returning it to its country of origin? Right? Of course that wouldn't matter, and she knew it.

The sun was setting, and she still had about two hours to reach the site. She was so exhausted, her thoughts drifted between fantasy and reality. She would be too tired to set up her tent and would have to sleep in the car. That was fine. No one was around for miles. It was what Jen loved about the desert. It was what she loved about her work. The isolation was a comfort to her, but if something happened out here, she'd be on her own to deal with it.

With the darkness came the cold. Jen always preferred that to the heat of midday, although this time of year it rarely broke ninety degrees. A few months earlier, it would have been too hot to bring Dugg. Still, it was easier to stay warm than to cool off. She drove another hour and then turned off the car.

"We're sleeping here tonight, bud. Can't keep my eyes open." Jen opened the glove compartment and pulled out the flute. She unwrapped it and gave it yet another inspection, checking for any damage from the travel. It was okay. She set it on her lap and rested her head on the headrest. *So tired...* She put her seat back and immediately fell asleep.

***

"And there came a goblin whose breath was fire," said a man. Jen knew he was Eaden the bard, come to teach the children. *I'm still in Scotland,* she thought. *Thirteen hundreds?* In her dreams, it was difficult to gauge the exact year, but she was always able to backtrack to figure it out when she woke. And she wasn't Jen, but Gavina. She sat in the grass listening to the lively tales told by old Eaden.

"He played his harp till the village folk slept. Except for one brave warrior..."

Jen/Gavina looked side to side. Four boys and two girls sat around her. She knew each of them and played with them every day. *They've been dead for more than half a millenium*, the Jen-half of her thought, morbidly. The rain fell lightly, but they stayed dry beneath a fat tree, thick with leaf.

"That one man, who went by the name Fionn the Fair, fought the mortal slumber by breathing the foouuul poison from his magic spear!"

"Oooo," went the children, including Gavina.

"The poison did'nae kill him?" asked Owen.

"No, it did'nae!" said Eaden. "It would take more'n that to kill a man with… *all the knowledge of the land!*"

"Wait," said Sophie. "How can a harp put a whole village to sleep?"

"Goblins can do some mingin' bad things! And this was a right bad one! Aillen was its name. T'would burn down the halls of Tara every year."

"A goblin set my da's woodcart afire," said Ian.

"Aye, one did at that," said the bard. "But that was not Aillen, for ye see, he was killed by Fionn and his poison spear. He was a hero and was given a band of great warriors. They—"

***

Dugg barked and woke Jen. She cleared the fog from her window and looked out into the desert. A rabbit hopped a few feet away.

"Easy, Dugg," she said. "I wish you had let me find out how the story ended." She scratched the dog behind his ears. This, had been a tough few days for him, too. He didn't enjoy his time in the crate in the cargo area of the plane. When she travelled, she usually had someone come to the house to feed him and take him for walks. This time, though, she wasn't sure when she was coming back. She wasn't sure *if* she was coming back. When they were reunited in the terminal, his crate was filled with hair shed from the stress of the trip.

Jen reached into the back seat and pulled a biscuit from the box and flipped it to him. She looked at the clock. She'd only slept for an hour. *Are the police at my door back home now? Would Hirnhoff have really called them on me?* Not that he shouldn't have. But she really hoped he was only bluffing. It was hard to imagine him actually doing it. Just as it was hard to imagine herself in handcuffs, or behind bars.

"Do you think you could crunch any *louder*?" she asked her dog. Then she noticed something through the window behind him. Car lights!

"*No!*" she shouted. Who would be out here at this hour? Or at all? Were they looking for her? They *had* to be!

Jen turned the key and started the car. She stepped on the gas and rolled into the darkness ahead, headlights off so she wouldn't give away her location. There was no road, but the sand was fairly stable in this part of the desert. She'd have to avoid cacti and other thorny plants that sprung up. And, of course, low, tire-popping rocks, which were everywhere. The half-moon shed just enough light to reveal the shapes of the obstacles moments before she came upon them. She drove with her face practically pressed into the windshield. With only an hour's sleep in two days, she wasn't thinking clearly, and those obstacles seemed to be coming at her more and more quickly. But she strongly suspected that the person, or people, behind those lights were not friends. *Or am I just paranoid?* Jen looked down and saw the flute perched on her lap. She grabbed it with one hand and wrapped it back up as she steered around the desert flora and placed it on the floor behind her.

Dugg was restless and circled in his seat. He knew something was wrong and whined loudly.

"It's okay, boy," said Jen. "It's okay." It wasn't, though, and dogs don't listen to words, they hear how they're spoken. She looked in her rearview mirror and saw the lights. They were still a good distance away. If they were following her, they weren't going any faster than she was. Off to her left was an old riverbed channel, filled by water during the periodic rains, the last ones having done so over two years ago. It would be bone dry now.

"Hang on, Dugg!" She steered down into the ravine, hoping to bring her car below the horizon and out of sight from her pursuer. The sand was packed more tightly here, and she could drive a little faster.

After about twenty minutes, she stopped and turned off the engine.

"Stay here," she said to the dog, and climbed out of the car. She walked up the shallow bank and searched the dimly lit desert. At the very edge of her sight, she saw the lights. They had continued in a different direction, moving away from her. Jen climbed down and went back to her car. She let Dugg out to do his business and then the two of them climbed back inside.

"I think we're okay," she said. *Were they actually following me? Maybe they were here for a different reason. But what would possibly bring someone way out here?*

Jen started the car and began to drive up the sandy bank. She got halfway up when the Jeep got stuck.

"*No! No! No!*" She put it in four-wheel low and tried again, and again. When the car failed to budge, she went out to see how much trouble she was in.

"*Nooo!*" she shouted and kicked the bumper. All four tires were buried to the axles in the sand. She got back in the car and slumped in her seat. Dugg licked her face nervously, and she ignored it, staring ahead into the sand that entrapped them. Jen grabbed her phone, but knew it was useless. There would be no signal for miles. *But maybe...* No, there was no maybe, and no signal. She wanted to scream. She wanted even more to cry, but there wasn't enough energy left in her body to do either.

"Lie down, Dugg," she said. The dog took his paws off the center console and curled up in his seat. His eyes never left her, though. "Be right back."

Jen got out of the car again and stumbled up the embankment. She scanned the horizon. The lights were gone. No one would be able to see her in the ravine, anyway. That was both good and bad. She walked back to the car. The situation looked hopeless. She might be able to prop up one side with the jack, but then what? *Too tired to think. Will look again in the morning.* The problem was every minute out in this arid wilderness was a minute she might need to escape. She dropped to the sand and leaned against the fender. Suddenly, she felt an intense burning in her ankle. The pale moon illuminated a little yellow scorpion, about to sting her a second time.

Chapter 20

Bulo began to shake.

"*Get up! Everyone!*" shouted Skeetu.

"He's going to—?" began Hanna.

"*Yes! Run!*"

The six had spent the night with the woolly rhino. They wound up partially buried in snow, but his body kept them warmer than if they had stayed in the cave. They sprung to their feet and plowed into the snow in six directions. Bulo was now up, running in circles, plunging his massive horn into unseen targets.

"Get behind a tree, Chup!" shouted Skeetu. "He has no control!" The sahaar had stopped to watch the great spearnose but was too close to him. He turned and hobbled further away and dropped low to the ground.

Bulo circled five times and then stopped. He looked around him and saw Skeetu come out from behind a rock.

"It's over, everyone," she announced. She and the rhino walked to one another. He looked at her as if nothing had happened. She rubbed his shoulder as she inspected his batbear wounds.

"You will be all right," she said. "Thank you for keeping them away from us." Soohla and Rin pushed through the snow to join them.

"Is he hurt?" asked the girl.

"Yes," said the oldkin, "But he will heal. The wounds are not deep."

Rin pointed to the surrounding forest.

"They will be back. I know," she said.

"But will we still be here?" asked Soohla.

Haana had been walking in a wide circle around them, kicking at the snow. She joined the other three.

"Have you ever eaten batbear?" she asked. "There is one for each of us." They all shook their heads.

"I don't think they taste good," said Soohla. "Eaters of old meat…" Rin made a disgusted face.

"It is food, though," said Haana. "They will not poison us, I don't think."

"Where's Chup? And Dami?" asked Soohla.

Rin pointed to the cave. The four walked toward it. Skeetu reached out to the rhino and pulled his fur.

"Come," she said. "Wait by the opening." Surprisingly, he came with her.

They walked inside. Now that it was morning, it was easier to see inside the cave. The oldkin found the drawings on the wall to be unsettling. Not frightening, or disturbing; she just wasn't sure what to make of them.

"I am useless," said Chup, sitting on the floor and staring at his hands. "These fingers… can't even hold a spear."

Dami was at the far side, going through her pouch. She found a tuber she had dug up two days ago and bit into it. From the look on her face, it was still frozen. She held it between her hands to thaw it out. For a while, no one said anything.

"Have you ever eaten batbear?" asked Soohla.

Chup huffed. "I have."

"Because there are a lot of dead ones out there. We can probably turn them into enough food to get us to the scrubhills," said Hanna. "Rin has been both pushing through the trail and hunting food for us. Maybe now he won't have to hunt. But we'll have to cut it up before the meat freezes too hard."

"Scrubhills? That is not happening," said the old man. "It's still snowing. Have you looked outside? This is where it ends for us."

"For you, maybe," said Dami.

"For all of us, girl," snapped Chup. "Too much water in the snow. We will get wet through our hides and freeze. This I do know."

"Maybe not," said Skeetu. "I do not want to see the other sahaar. I am not sure they would take me in, but I have traveled in this snow many times. Bulo pushes through in front and makes a path. It is lumpy walking, but it can be done."

"What else would we do?" asked Haana. "Stay here? How much farther to… I forgot where we are going…"

"Scrubhills," said Soohla.

"Scrubhills, yes," said Haana. "I was asking you something…"

"I think we are four days away from the foot of them, which is as far as I have gone," said Skeetu. "The scrubhills, another day or two after that? It depends on the weather. I've only done this once, so I'm not sure."

"If we stay here, the snow will probably get worse instead of better," said Soohla.

"And if it gets worse while you are in the open," said Chup, "It is over."

Rin slapped his chest and pointed outdoors to indicate he wanted to keep moving. He gestured to the trees outside and then to a dead hyena on the floor.

"Yes, I think we should, too," said Haana. "Those batbears will be back. I do not want to fight them again. I would rather eat the dead ones on our way out of here, than be eaten by those hungry for sahaar."

"We should go," agreed Soohla. Dami nodded.

"I'm staying until there is a break in the snow," said Chup. "I have not lived this long life by chasing foolish decisions. So far, every choice I have made has kept me breathing! *Every* one!"

"What if the batbears come? They will, you know," said Soohla.

"I have some time to build a fire. That will keep them away," said the old man.

"Until you go for more wood outside," said the girl. "You were just saying that you couldn't hold a spear! If you stay here, you are saying to us, 'Now go, while I feed the batbears'."

"I am staying until the weather clears," repeated Chup. "This I know and will not be told I do not."

The group collected and slaughtered the dead cave hyenas. Dami had the idea of hanging their sacks of meat on Bulo's back.

"I don't think he will like it," said Skeetu. "And how would we keep it from slipping off?"

"There is a way," said the sahaar. "I will think about it while I haul this heavy sack of horrid meat on my back."

"You could leave it behind anytime," said Soohla. "But you can't have mine when you're hungry."

"Chup said it won't taste good anyway," said Dami.

"It will when you have gone a while without food," said Haana.

It was time to leave. Bulo led the way, pushing through the snow along the edge of the ravine. The others walked behind him. Rin went first, since he was the largest of the group and would pack down the path better than the others. Last, being the smallest, was Dami, who had the benefit of a trail made by the group in front of her.

"I will catch up," said Skeetu and she turned back and headed for the cave. Chup had gathered some sticks for a fire and was about to go out for more.

"Changed your mind, old kind?" he asked.

"No," said Skeetu. "I wanted to ask you something. The whisperflute… were you telling me the truth about it?"

"I do not lie. I told you what I knew—what I heard," said the old man.

"And you believe it? All of it?"

"Yes."

"I want to find the sticklegs. I will find it!"

"Remember, you cannot kill it. You must comfort it in its death. Who will make the flute if you cannot?"

"I will figure it out. I hope you will be okay here," said the oldkin.

"I do, too," said Chup. "But I would rather wait here, warm and dry than freeze out in the snow. And get eaten by things meaner than batbears. There are things worse than dying in a warm cave. Now either stay and gather some wood or catch up with the others."

Skeetu heard that as 'goodbye'. She left the cave and followed the trail back to her friends. She knew she would never see him again.

***

The traveling was slow, and arduous. The snow was up to Skeetu's waist. If it weren't for Bulo, they would have been forced to wait in the cave with Chup. The oldkin wondered if she would have been better off doing that, not because of the weather, but because of where they were headed. That she was accepted by the sahaar with her was no guarantee the ones ahead would do the same. She secretly hoped they would never be found and that they would live as a small clan of their own. Rin would be their new leader. He was strong and knew when to be cautious, and when to charge ahead, as he did with the batbears. Skeetu found that thoughts of Rin put her at ease. While he was not outwardly friendly, he was never unfriendly, either. And she trusted him. He seemed to be learning to trust her, too.

The snow stopped falling by early evening. They had not traveled as far as they had hoped. Bulo had little trouble pushing through, but he also had no interest in walking any faster than he was inclined to go.

The group came to a stop. The sky was clear, glowing with the countless lights of Skeetu's ancestors. *Someday I will play my songs for you,* she thought. *But first I must find that special bird.* The oldkin wasn't worried about that. She believed that she would be able to track down the sticklegs. She was more concerned about making a flute from its bone. It was something she had yet been able to do, but she would. *This I do know,* she thought, thinking of Chup.

While it was a relief to see the clouds move on, it also meant that the evening air would be very cold. The wind had died down some, but there was enough of a steady breeze to carry that chill through her body. They found themselves in front of a huge snowdrift that had collected in the corner of two large boulders.

"We should tunnel in," said the oldkin, "It will get us out of the wind."

They set to digging and in time had hollowed out two cavities large enough for all of them to squeeze inside. They were soaking wet, not so much from the snow, but the sweat from digging. Rin dropped an armful of sticks between the entrances and started a fire with his striking stones. The rest of them collected some larger branches to feed the flames and soon they were gathered around it, hands out to warm their frozen fingers.

"Not a lot of wood around," said Soohla. "This will be a short fire."

"It's going to be tight in that snow cave," said Dami.

"It would have been tighter if Chup had come," said Haana. "I think he made a mistake staying back there on his own."

"He will be dead by tomorrow," said Dami.

"You don't know that," scolded Soohla. Rin touched his chest and held his palms in the air.

"Yes," said the girl. "We might be, too."

Skeetu played her flute for a while. It seemed to quiet everyone's thoughts.

"The fire is getting low. I'm cold," said Dami.

"We should sleep," said Soohla. "Rin only has room for two in his shelter, so I am guessing Haana will go with him. And we three will squeeze into ours."

"I want to go with Rin," said Dami. "And Haana," she added. "I will feel safer with him. And her…"

"Did you see Skeetu jump on that batbear's back?" asked Soohla. "I think we will be better off with her!" Dami said nothing. She pushed past the other sahaar girls and squeezed into their shelter.

"We can switch, if you want," said Haana to her brother. Rin shook his head.

"Bulo, stay with us. Do not wander," the oldkin said to the spearnose. Bulo walked away and disappeared around an outcropping of rocks. She and Soohla joined Dami in the snow cave.

"He listens well," said Soohla. "I hope he doesn't get—"

"He won't," said Skeetu. But she was worried about him wandering in the night.

"Tie his horn to a tree," suggested Dami.

"I think that's a great idea, Dami!" said Soohla. "And I think you should be the one to do it, too!" The girl sniffed and rolled away from the other two. She was snoring moments later. The other two were right behind her.

Chapter 21

"Move your leg," said Dami.

"Me?" asked Skeetu.

"Your leg is against mine."

"So? It's tight in here. Soohla's leg is touching your other leg. Her arm was in my face half the night."

"It is different. I do not like to be touched."

"By an *oldkin*, yes?"

Dami was silent a moment. "Hush. I have to get out of here."

"We all do," said Soohla, awakened by the bickering in the snow shelter.

The three squeezed out into the open. Judging by the sun, it was late morning. The extra rest was welcome after the restless night before.

"Haana! Rin! Come on!" shouted Soohla. The brother and sister sleepily crawled out to join the others.

"It is late," said Soohla. "We slept a long time."

"Needed to," said Haana, yawning.

"Sssst!" hissed Rin. He pointed to some tracks in the snow.

"Wolf!" said Skeetu. "It was right outside where we were sleeping!"

"Why didn't it attack?" asked Dami.

"Skeetu, you don't think…" began Haana.

"I don't know," said the oldkin. "Why would it come all the way here?"

Rin raised his hands in question. He didn't know about the wolf she referred to.

"Skeetu's friend," answered Haana. "It lives outside her camp back in the needletree forest. I never saw it, but we'd often hear its footsteps in the leaves along the edges. And Skeetu would hear it howling at night."

"I have seen it. A big male," said Skeetu. "But I don't know if it is my *friend*, Haana. It just stays around. The last few nights I've been hearing a howling wolf, but far away. You all hear it, too, yes?" Rin nodded. The others had not, though.

"It is a long way from home," said Haana.

"So are we," said Soohla. "Where's Bulo?"

"Do you think the wolf…" suggested Dami.

"No," said the oldkin. "A single wolf could not take him down." She called out to the spearnose. Rin pointed to the animal's trail, which led away from their overnight stop. They gathered their things and set out to catch up with him. They didn't have to walk far. Up ahead, Bulo had his head buried in the snow. When he heard the others coming, he pulled it free, and looked at them, still chewing on the plants he'd managed to uncover.

"Show us the way, spearnose," said Haana. Bulo had grown nearly as close to the sahaar girl as he had to

Skeetu and ignored her just the same. He stuck his head back in the snow to search for more food.

"We may be a while," said the oldkin.

"Do you think Chup made it through the night?" asked Haana.

"Probably not," said Dami.

"If the batbears came back, the fire should have kept them away," said Soohla.

"He will have to keep it burning for a long time," said Haana. "This was all his idea, and then he decides to stay behind?"

"I think it was too hard for him," said Soohla. "He didn't complain much, but I could hear his knees clicking, louder and louder."

"I heard that, too," said Skeetu. "I hope that someday we see him again. But…"

"I doubt he survived the night," said Dami.

"Yes, you would doubt that," said Soohla.

Bulo finished his breakfast and pushed through the snow. It was another clear day, and much welcomed by the group. The rhino's path led down a sloping hill, which he navigated by zigzagging back and forth to keep from losing his footing. The others would have made it down faster, each able to handle steep hills better than the front-heavy wooly rhino, but they were dependent upon his leading the way and had no choice but to follow.

That night, they made camp in a wooded valley. Rin built the fire, and the others prepared their evening meal. There was still some elk left, so they didn't need to dig into the batbears yet, which was a relief to all of them, although none of them had yet to try it.

Rin finished eating and sat, absently grooming the two red feathers that hung from his spear.

"Why do you tie those to your spear?" asked Skeetu.

Rin's hands mimicked a bird's flapping wings. Then he drew a long arc in the air.

"It makes it fly higher! Like a bird! Would feathers work for my spear?"

The sahaar nodded confidently. He glanced up to the sky and stood. A concerned look crossed his face and he pointed up to the gathering clouds.

"Another storm coming, yes," said Soohla. "I saw that."

"This was not the best time to be making this trip," said Dami.

"Did we have another choice?" asked Soohla.

"We… where are we going?" asked Haana.

Dami rolled her eyes. "Scrubhills! Scrubhills!" she said, impatiently.

"Okay! I know!" said Haana. "I forget things since…" She chose not to finish that sentence. Skeetu looked down at her feet and said nothing. Rin shoved Dami's shoulder hard and gave her a stern look.

"I'm sorry," she said. "I'm sorry, Haana. I know the old kind's… sneak attack… did something to your head. It is not your fault."

"Would you play for us tonight, my friend?" Haana asked Skeetu. "We are in a dark way. Your music helps us find a better place.

The oldkin did not feel like playing her flute. Every time Haana forgot what she should have remembered, she was reminded of the terrible thing she did. She shook her head no. Soohla stood up and grabbed a short stick.

"I don't know why no one ever asks me!" she said. She held the stick to her mouth and danced around the fire, humming a silly tune through her nose. Skeetu, Rin, and Haana laughed. Dami released a tiny, reluctant smile.

"Come on, Skeetu! Join me!" The oldkin pulled out her flute and played along with her friend's comical romp. Then Rin leapt to his feet and galloped around the fire with his spear, poking the air like Bulo in one of his fits. Their laughter exploded; even Dami couldn't hold it back. Soohla stopped and sat down, out of breath. Rin dropped down next to her. Skeetu had never seen such joy in his face. It made her feel lighter than a puff of air.

"We have not laughed since the valley," said Soohla. "It feels wrong."

"No," said Haana. "It does not feel wrong. Why are we fighting to live if we cannot find a laugh inside?"

They built the fire up high and spent the night out in open. The storm arrived before first light. Skeetu woke beneath a light blanket of snow. Rin was already laying more branches onto the dying embers. There was anxiousness in his face. *This is going to be a bad one,* she thought. *He knows it, too.* He looked at the oldkin and made a comforting gesture. *We will be all right;* he was telling her. And at that moment, she believed him. Then the sahaar held up a finger, asking Skeetu to wait. He went and got his spear and returned. It was missing one of the bright red feathers, which he held in his hand. He handed it to her and then pointed to the oldkin's spear.

"This is for me?" she asked. He nodded. Skeetu did not know what to say. Dami walked up to them.

"Won't work for yours, I don't think," she said. The oldkin ignored her. She was picturing her spear flying through the air like a hawk. Rin's spear flew ahead of hers, dipping and diving in the air.

It was time to leave. Bulo was with them, for a change, so they didn't have to go searching for their guide. They gathered their packs and set out into the howling white swirl before them. No one spoke. The wind was so loud, their words would have been lost, anyway.

The group pushed through for several hours. Skeetu was up front this time, followed by Haana, and then Soohla. Rin and Dami had fallen back. Normally, Rin took the lead to tramp down the snow for the others. Since the wolf, however, he felt the need to bring up the rear, in case it came upon them from behind. Skeetu was not concerned about the wolf, though. It had never given her a reason to feel unsafe, despite having many opportunities to attack. *That might not be 'my' wolf, though.*

"I need to stop for a little bit," Haana shouted over the snow-packed gusts.

"Up ahead," shouted Skeetu. "I see a fallen tree. We can use it to block the wind."

They trudged forward and dropped down against the massive trunk. The sudden silence was as powerful as the roar of the wind.

"Where's my brother?" asked Haana.

"He's coming," said Soohla.

"Where? When did you last see him?"

"I don't know. A while ago. He and Dami will catch up."

The three waited, searching the churning wall of white for movement. Minutes passed. Then an hour. Skeetu expected to see their outlines at any moment, but no one appeared.

"They're lost," said Haana. "Or…"

The oldkin knew what she was thinking, but she wouldn't say it aloud. *Wolf.*

"We don't know that Haana," said Soohla. "They may be tucked in somewhere. They will catch up."

"I will find them," said Skeetu.

"*No!*" said Haana. "We will lose you, too!"

"This storm is not as bad for my kind as it is yours," said the oldkin. "We do not get as cold. I will find them."

"I will come with you," said Soohla.

"No, stay with Haana. You would slow me down."

Skeetu pressed into the snow. *There are not a lot of places for them to go. They would have to walk off the deep path to get lost.* The thought returned to her. One she quickly buried. *The wolf.* The wind picked up and nearly knocked her off her feet. She was used to the snow, but this was worse than anything she'd ever experienced. The oldkin followed their trail, which was quickly filling in. If she wasn't careful, she'd be unable to find her way back. She searched for a very long time, nearly making it halfway back to where they started. Suddenly, her foot dropped down into a hole. Without thinking, she dove forward, facedown into the unpacked snow. Skeetu rolled over and looked behind her. There was a steep cliff adjacent to Bulo's trail. *We could have all slid down there so easily!* Then she had a horrifying thought. *Did Rin and Dami fall down there?*

Skeetu cautiously pulled herself to the edge and looked down. It was a straight drop for as far as she could see. Hanging from the branches of a small shrub that hugged the wall was an elk skin bag. *Rin's!* She tried to reach it, but realized it was too dangerous on the slippery rim. She worked her way back, and then stopped. Rin's bag held his striking stones. Without them, they would all freeze to death. Dami had two of her own, but where was she?

The oldkin went back to the edge, reached out with her spear, and hooked the bag. Then, with great care, she freed it from the branch and brought it back to the trail. *How will I tell Haana? How will I...* She was crying. It was not something she could remember doing since her family was killed by the cave bear so long ago. Rin was a good sahaar. A good sahaar *man*. He was brave, and strong, and looked out for them all. *He gave me a flying feather!* She had recognized a while back that Rin was Leader, not Chup. Chup thought of Chup, but Rin thought of the others before he thought of Rin. She didn't realize how much she thought of him until that moment. *He gave me a flying feather.* It meant more to her than any gift she had ever received. Now he was gone. The tears were freezing on her lashes, making it harder to work her way back. *Dami will be gone, too,* she thought. The sahaar was always by Rin's side, whether he liked it or not. Dami was difficult to like, but she was part of her new clan. Skeetu would laugh with joy if she came bounding down the trail.

But she did not.

The oldkin cradled the pouch in her arms and fought her way back to her friends. They began as six. Now they were three.

Chapter 22

Haana lay curled in a ball against the fallen tree that sheltered the girls from the wind. Soohla rubbed her shoulder, not knowing what else to do, or say. Skeetu sat nearby. She wanted to help her friend, but like Soohla, did not know how. And she was not sahaar and felt she should not intrude on sahaar pain. Haana had now lost the last of her family. Rin was her protector. But more importantly, he was her silent confidant. The loss left the three of them sapped of will. They no longer wished to seek out the clan in the scrubhills. They had no desire to return to where they started, either. They accepted they would be trapped in this dire moment until the snow rose up and buried them. Then Haana would join her brother in the deep valley. Soohla would be there, too. And all of their family and friends who died in the sickness. Skeetu feared she would never see her friends again, as the sahaar did not travel to the lights in the sky when their breaths were stilled. If given the choice, would she pick the deep valley over the stars? She didn't know. Maybe. But likely not. She hoped she would not be forced to choose.

It was Soohla who broke the silence. She stood and looked back toward where they came from, hoping to see Rin or Dami appear on the trail. There was just snow and wind.

"We should go," she said.

"Where?" asked Skeetu.

"To the scrubhills."

"Haana?" asked Skeetu.

"I don't know," said the sahaar. "I don't really care any more."

"No, you do not right now," said Soohla, "But you will. Otherwise, this would have been for nothing."

"You two go," said her friend.

"Not without you. And Skeetu," she added. "We're not going to just lie here and freeze. I'm not going to let that happen!"

"There is a thick forest ahead, I think," said Skeetu. "If we make it there before it gets too dark, we will be out of the wind." The other two nodded. The oldkin pushed Bulo forward and they continued their journey.

Skeetu was right about the forest. It was not very far ahead. The wind began to die down, as did the snowfall. They found a somewhat clear area that was sheltered by tall trees. Skeetu started a fire with Rin's stones. They sat in silence and finished the rest of the elk meat, although Haana ate nothing.

"Dami is happy now," she said, after a while.

"Yes," said Soohla. "She is with who she wanted to be with."

"You knew this?" asked Skeetu.

"You did not?" asked Soohla.

"No, I did. I never knew Dami the way you two did. She did not like me."

"It did seem that way at times," said Soohla. "There was always something different about her. I don't know what. She sometimes acted like she wanted to be with us, but when she was, it seemed like she wanted to be somewhere else."

"You don't know where she came from?" asked Skeetu.

"No one does, except her father, of course."

"She did come to visit you," said Haana. "How much could she hate you?"

"She came because you two did," answered the oldkin. Then she added, "I will miss your brother."

"Me, too," said Soohla. Haana nodded.

"I will get more wood," said Skeetu. She was afraid she would begin to cry again and didn't want them to see it. She stood and left the fire. She could hear the girls talking and paused to listen.

"Without Rin, and Chup, the sahaar might not take in Skeetu," said Soohla.

"I know," said Haana.

"We are just girls. Our word will not carry as theirs would."

"I know."

"So what do we do?"

"I don't know."

"They will see she is not sahaar," said Soohla.

"They will," said Haana, "But if we are going there, we need her help."

"I know."

"Maybe they will accept her. We have. We will convince them, somehow."

The words Skeetu heard from her friends grew inside her like a block of ice. She was not *them*. She would never be *them*. After all that had happened, and all she had done for them in friendship, they would always be sahaar and she would always be oldkin. She wanted to run off and not come back. Leave them here in the woods. After the shock of losing Rin, this was more than she could bear.

But Skeetu was oldkin. Oldkin acted. They did not lay out long and tangled plans. Oldkin moved on their thoughts. She tromped back to the fire and looked down at the two girls.

"Why should I lead you to a place where I will be chased away?" she asked.

They both seemed startled. "You heard us," said Haana, quietly.

"You would let me go to the sahaar when you know I will not be accepted among them?"

"No!" said Haana. "No! We want you with us! Not because of Bulo, but because you are our friend! We will beg them to take you with us!"

"You are our friend," said Soohla. "You are our… sister!"

Skeetu laughed. "*Your sister*. How can that be? Look at me! It is clear I am not one of you!"

Haana stood and walked up to the oldkin. She wrapped her arms around her and hugged her tightly. The sahaar said nothing while Skeetu stood there, arms pinned to her sides, not knowing what to do. Soohla stood and joined Haana. The two held their oldkin friend for what seemed to her a very long time. No one had ever done that, hugged her. She had seen the sahaar do it, but it was not an oldkin thing. It was frightening, but at the same their warmth melted the ice in her chest.

"It is a hard time for all of us," said Haana, letting go. Soohla did the same.

"We are together," said Soohla.

"Those are nice words," said Skeetu, "But the words you said before frighten me."

"We are afraid," said Haana. "Sometimes when we are afraid, we throw words into the wind—foolish words. We don't know if they will accept us, either. We are all risking that they will."

"And if they do not?"

"I don't know. What would you have us do? What would *you* do?"

Skeetu tried to give her an answer. It was a very important question; one that had been asked off and on since they set out on this quest.

Finally, she said, "I don't know, either."

Soohla spoke up. "Rin did not want to do this at first, but that changed after a time. I trust him... *trusted* him. He knew you were with us, Skeetu, and he still wanted to push forward. Do you think he believed you would be turned away to live on your own?"

"Maybe," said Skeetu. "I don't know what he thought. But without him, as you said, they might turn me away."

"What should we do?" asked Haana. "I will do what you say. I don't want to do this as much as I did at first. But… I will do what you say."

"I will, too," said Soohla.

The oldkin sighed. "We keep going. But do not make it Haana, Soohla, and the oldkin. We are Haana, Soohla, and Skeetu."

"We are," said Haana.

"We are," said Soohla.

***

They continued on the next morning. The sky had cleared, and the new terrain had not received as much snow as where they'd come from. As they rounded the corner, Soohla let out an excited whoop.

"There they are!" she said. "It is how Chup described them—the scrubhills!"

In the distance lay a vast open expanse, dotted by low-growing shrubs for as far as they could see. Before that was a series of folds in the land, valleys and hills, the foothills Skeetu had visited with Bulo some time ago. Where they stood was still blanketed in snow, but it was now barely up to their knees. The air was still, and warmer than it had been. The girls shed a layer of their mammoth hides.

"Do you see anyone, Skeetu?" asked Soohla.

The oldkin scanned the area. Nothing was moving. She knew any sahaar seen from this distance would be a tiny speck.

"No," she said.

"Smoke would tell us they are here," said Haana.

"No smoke," said Skeetu.

"They might be in a valley on the other side," said Soohla. "We should be able to get there in two days."

The two sahaar seemed excited. Skeetu was not. She would learn soon whether or not she'd be going back to living on her own, with Bulo.

***

The trek to the foothills was uneventful, and quiet. While they saw a possible end to their journey, the loss of Rin and Dami was a heavy weight for the three of them. They reached a shallow valley by night and built a fire.

"I wish they were here," said Haana.

"I do, too," said Skeetu.

"I still feel a strong hurt from what happened in our valley, but this one is worse. I don't think it will go away."

"It won't," said Skeetu.

165

"You sound like Dami," said Soohla.

"It won't go away, Soohla. It just won't."

"Yes, you would know," said Haana.

"Once we get to… where we are going, I am going to find a stickleg. It will bring them back to me."

"Will it?" asked Soohla. "Uncle, and Chup, said it sings to the fallen in the deep valley. Will you be able to hear *them*, though?"

"I will find out," said the oldkin. She took out her flute. "I have a song for Rin. It has been growing inside me as we walked. Can I play it?"

"I don't know, Skeetu," said Haana. "I don't know if I can hear it."

"Another time, then"

"Okay."

Bulo had gone as far as he was going to. He was done leading. Just beneath the snow was a grand stretch of succulent greens, which was all he showed any interest in. As far as he was concerned, they had reached the end.

"Now what do we do?" asked Haana.

"We don't need to follow him any more," said Soohla. "I think we can reach the top before dark and see if we see anything."

"I will stay with Bulo," said Skeetu.

"No! You come with us!" insisted Haana.

"No, you don't need me up there. If you see anyone, come down and let me know. I will wait."

"Are you sure?" asked Soohla. She was having a hard time containing her impatience.

"Go. I will wait."

The sahaar rushed up the hills and were soon tiny dots in the distance. Skeetu opened her sack and chewed on a bit of batbear she had cooked earlier. It was tough, with a strong, sour flavor, but it was food. By the end of the day, she saw the girls rushing down the hills. The oldkin grabbed her spear and stood. *Are they being chased?*

She met them part of the way up. Night had fallen, dark and moonless. She could see their shapes, though, getting closer. No one seemed to be following them. Haana and Soohla practically crashed into the oldkin, unable to stop. They were too out of breath to speak at first.

"Sahaar…" said Soohla "Many, many… sahaar!"

"We saw… them," added Haana. "They… did… not see… us."

"Do they look friendly?" asked Skeetu. She was both happy for them, and afraid of what lay ahead.

"Cannot… say. Many children," said Soohla. "So that… might… be good."

"What do we do now?" asked the oldkin.

"We go to them tomorrow," said Haana.

"We are home," said Soohla.

You *are home*, thought Skeetu.

Chapter 23

Jen kicked at the scorpion with her other foot, and it scuttled away, slipping under a nearby rock. Her ankle was on fire. She stood and yanked open the door to the car. Dugg was sitting at attention in his seat. The flute was in his mouth. *I can't believe this!*

"Dugg," she said, trying to sound calmer than she was. "Dugg, drop it. Drop it?" Dugg panted, the flute still tucked into his back teeth. Drool dripped off the end.

"No, Duggy. No bone." She felt behind the seat, keeping her eyes on the dog, and grabbed a biscuit. "Here you go. Biscuit? Wanna biscuit?"

Jen held the treat under his nose so he could smell it and slowly reached forward. She gently placed her fingers on the end of the bone flute. Her ankle felt like it was being stung over and over, but she knew the scorpion was gone. She also knew that all the dog had to do was chomp down just the tiniest bit, and this whole crazy journey would be over.

"Here, Dugg. Biscuit?"

The dog opened his mouth a little and she slid out the slobber-covered flute. Jen gave it a quick look and it seemed undamaged. She could not imagine what she would have done had she returned to find it chewed to pieces!

There was still the matter of the scorpion sting. She grabbed a flashlight and looked at her ankle. It was starting to swell. It felt like invisible scorpions were still stinging her. Hives popped up in reaction to the venom, climbing up her calf. She reached into a bag in the back seat, fished out her emergency medical kit, and popped a couple of antihistamines in her mouth. They would make her sleepy, but it would help counter an allergic reaction.

She looked over at Dugg. "Ever have one of those days?" She laughed. What else was there to do at this point? She was jobless. Police were likely ransacking her apartment. She was stranded in a desert in Spain. A scorpion envenomated her ankle moments ago. And her dog had been just a hiccup away from destroying the thing that drove all this.

Jen climbed into the back the seat and put her foot up on the center console. She knew to elevate the ankle to keep the swelling down. The antihistamines began to kick in, reducing some of the throbbing, and pain. They also put her to sleep.

***

She woke a few times throughout the night, but quickly nodded off again. In the morning, the low sun shone through the windows. Jen looked at her ankle. There was just a slight bumpy area where she'd been attacked. The whole experience had been like a bad hornet sting.

"I survive," she said to Dugg. She climbed out of the car and let her dog out the door. Jen scanned the ground for rogue scorpions, but knew they wouldn't be out in the open, especially in the daylight. "I guess they are not deadly," she said. *What to do now?* She debated whether or not to stay with the vehicle, which is what you're supposed to do in this situation. *Or was that just for capsized boats? Do I hike back to civilization?* It was clear the Jeep was staying right where it was. She had water and food, having stocked up in a bodega just before setting out into the desert. *I kind of wish I didn't lose the car that was out there last night,* she thought. The more she considered it, the less likely it seemed it had anything to do with her.

In the end, she chose neither of those two options. *In for a penny, in for a pound*, she thought. *I'm going to the site.* She'd remembered there were two full water jugs buried near the dig, just for emergencies. She had Dr Hirnhoff to thank for that. He said it was a crime to waste water in a desert, even if you brought more than you thought you needed. The cache of water was part of what steered her toward that decision. There would be none along the way had she set out for the nearest town. Plus, the dig was what brought her out here in the first place. She looked at her dog.

"Want to hear something really stupid, boy? We're going deeper into the desert! How about that?" Dugg wagged his tail.

Jen figured it would take her three hours on foot to reach Neandergirl's final resting place in the sand. If she left now, they'd arrive before the air grew too hot. She packed what she and Dugg would need and heaved the cumbersome burden onto her back. The dog's pack held some of her lighter digging equipment. She would have to be careful not to overburden him in the heat.

They reached the site without any new incidents and Jen set up the tarp to get them out of the sun. Everything was how she'd last left it. She filled Dugg's collapsible bowl with water, took a long drink herself, and sat a moment. *So, here I am again.* She unwrapped the flute and placed it, as she'd done in the past, where Neandergirl had rested. *It's home*, she said silently to the empty grave. Jen stood and walked in slow, ever-widening circles, looking for something to tip her off. She wasn't at all sure what she sought but knew that somewhere beneath the sand lay a clue to what this flute was doing to her. There was always more to find at these newer sites, and there was little doubt this was no exception. The heat was picking up and she stopped for a break in the shade of the tarp. She took back the flute and worked on clearing it out some more. She was almost all the way through. All that was left were a couple of plugged up spots that were harder to reach with her hand tools. *Oh, what will this sound like?* The anticipation was maddening, but she could not rush the delicate job. The archeologist decided to spend the hottest part of the day in the shade, picking away at the flute. She would continue her exploration when things cooled a bit.

"Dugg? This is where we belong. Do you know that?" The dog lay on his side and gave a lazy wag of his tail at hearing his name. He was panting but did not seem too bothered by the heat. *Why am I not panicking,* she wondered? *I have no idea how I'm getting out of this desert. The car is not going to magically free itself. No one is going to come by on a burro and offer us a ride home. If that happens, I'll know I've lost it! At some point I do have to leave. But how will I?* She held up the flute. *Oh, the trouble you cause.*

Some time ago, Jen had accepted that an inanimate object, *this* inanimate object, could completely take control of her life. The object was, in fact, anything but *inanimate,* though. It held a supernatural element or quality, or dare she think, *magic*? She had never believed in such things, but she had learned over the years to trust that which could be proven. *She* was the proof—her actions! Not just her dreams, which would have been enough to convince her something bigger was at play. No, it was the fact that she was powerless to give up the flute. Powerless, despite every logical and physical attempt to wrest it from herself. She could not do it! It made her wonder how she found it in the first place. When did it begin its pull on her? Back in the

States when she boarded the plane with Hirnhoff and the interns? When she first set foot in the desert? *When I was born?*

The flute had about an inch of blockage left to clear now. It would be only a few more hours. The joints in her fingers were sore from the work and she was stopping more frequently to rest them. Jen had a feeling that it needed to be played here, where the Neanderthal girl had died. Actually, she *knew* this. *Maybe that's why I'm here!* It did make sense to her logical side, which was comforting, after having been driven by so much *illogic* over the last few months. She decided to take another break and replaced the flute back where Neandergirl's hand had once held it—held it for 40,000 years.

The archeologist resumed her circles. She walked past where the woolly rhino horn was buried. There was no need to do much more with that. It was interesting but was not what she was looking for. Then she had an idea. She walked past the girl's resting place and peered down over the edge. It dropped off steeply at first, and then more gently as it met with the level desert sand. *Maybe something rolled down there.* She carefully climbed down over the ridge. *Scorpions. Scorpions. Scorpions,* she reminded herself, as she placed her hands where she could not see. Laying on her side, her body nearly vertical, she studied the surface of the rock. She ran her hand over it. Sometimes touch spoke louder than any visible clue. The sandstone had eroded over thousands of years, exposing the denser rocks trapped within. Her fingers fell upon one that was smooth and round.

"I don't think this was a riverbed," she said to herself. Rocks this shape were usually rounded by the water scouring them on a sandy bed.

Jen pulled herself closer to the object. She nearly screamed. She reached back into her shoulder bag and pulled out a flatknife and freed it from the surface. When she held it closer to her eyes, she did scream. She screamed over and over. Then she calmed herself, but realized her hands were shaking.

"Neandergirl! You did this?"

She was looking at a shell. Two holes were drilled in its edges, likely used to hang it from grass twine or a thin strip of leather. On its surface were thin carvings made with a fine stone tool.

Chapter 24

"Are you ready?" asked Soohla. She was practically vibrating with excitement. Haana and Skeetu were feeling more cautious, Skeetu, a considerable amount more than Haana.

"I think you two should go first. See if they accept you," said the oldkin.

"No," said Haana. "We started out together and we will finish together."

"I could be like a... an *animal* to them. I do not want to go. No. I am not going." Skeetu was wondering what she would do when the time finally came for her to present herself to the new sahaar. She envisioned many scenarios, but the one that visited her most frequently was the one that ended with spears in her ribs. Maybe it had something to do with the visual image Rin had put in her head. Nevertheless, it was not a foolish notion.

"You have to stay with us," said Haana.

"Come, Skeetu. They will like you like we do," added Soohla.

"How do you know this?"

"I just do. Come."

But Skeetu's mind was made. "No. You two go. If it goes well for you, ask them about me."

"That does make sense," said Soohla.

Haana reluctantly agreed. "Where will you be?" she asked.

"With Bulo. If you cannot find him when you return, then you do not have eyes."

"Or noses," joked Soohla.

"You may not come back. Remember, they attacked Chup."

"Any of them who attacked Chup are now too old to frighten me," said Soohla. The oldkin said nothing.

"We will come back for you, sister," said Haana.

Skeetu's heart soared at the word. *Sister.* She believed her. But her fear was not that she would be forgotten, it was that they would be killed or treated as enemies. She told them this already, though. And they knew it themselves. Rin certainly made sure they knew he thought it was possible, *likely* even. That they would risk their own lives to be with sahaar who could take those lives, taught her something about their people. It was a true need of theirs to be with their kind, and one they could not turn from.

Skeetu nodded and walked down the hill to find Bulo. There was nothing left for her to say. Soohla began to make her way toward the crest. Haana hesitated a moment, looking back at the oldkin, and then hurried to catch up.

The oldkin spent the day following Bulo around. This was an easier day than most, as the spearnose stayed in one general area. His belly had grown considerably, stuffed with the rich plants that grew in abundance. Skeetu kept an eye out for others of his kind, still wondering if this was where he came from. She thought she had seen some in the distance, but they were buffalos. From afar, they could easily have been mistaken for spearnoses, but for the lack of horns on their nose.

*****

Haana returned at the end of the day.

"Where is Soohla?" asked Skeetu.

"With them. Skeetu! They welcome us! They were happy to see us! They speak a little different, but we can make ourselves understood."

"That is good," said the oldkin. *Maybe*, she thought. "Are there any of… my kind there?"

"No," said the sahaar. "But we told them of you, and Bulo, and you can come, too!"

"Bulo, too?"

"Yes! But I don't think they really believed me."

"Or *maybe* they did not understand you. Haana?"

"No, Skeetu!"

"You know what I am going to say?"

"I do! And *no*, Skeetu!"

"I am not going," said the oldkin.

"Yes… you… *are*!" insisted the girl.

"No, I am not. I got you here. Bulo got you here, and I am happy you have found a new clan. I cannot join you yet. I have to find the sticklegs."

"Why? Why sing to the dead when you can sing with the living? With your friends? Your sisters?"

"I don't know why," said Skeetu. "I don't know why I brought you here, but I did. I don't know why I wander with a spearnose, but I do. I don't know why I need to find the bird, or to make a whisperflute, but I do! When I need to do a thing, I must do it until I have done it."

"I told Soohla you would say this," said Haana.

"I am sorry."

"No, do not be. I also told Soohla that if you do not return with me, I would stay with you. That I would try my best to convince you to come, but if I could not… if I could not… I think I said something else, but I don't remember."

"You did not tell her that!"

"I did! If you walk away, I walk away, too."

"Why would you do this?" asked the oldkin. She was elated that Haana said this, but she did not want to keep her from her sahaar.

"I thought I would want this more than I do, Skeetu. But I don't know if I am ready to start a new life yet. I am afraid to let go of my old one too soon because that would mean letting go of Rin. All of these terrible things *just* happened! Everything is moving and changing too fast! Rin and I were like… you and Bulo. We are… *were* … I forgot the words I was going to say…"

"No, that is okay. I know. But you do not have to forget him just because you are living with new sahaar."

"But that is what will happen! I have already begun to forget the sahaar from my valley! You know what… *happens* to me." She pointed to her head. "There will be so much new to me here. I will be too busy learning new ways… And I will forget. And then he will be gone from my thoughts forever on. I cannot do that to him."

"He will still be in mine, though, Haana."

Tears rolled down Haana's cheeks. "Yes," she said. "He will. And that is why I am going with you. I told myself after leaving Soohla that if we were moving on, I could hold on a little longer to those who I cared for. Those now in the deep valley—or up in your sky embers. Without you, I would not make it out here, alone, away from other sahaar. You are strong, and wise in the ways of the land. You see like a hawk. You have the ears of a hare, the strength of a bear. And you are my sister."

This nearly brought Skeetu to tears.

"If you had come to live with the sahaar," she continued, "then I would have, too. But now you have given me a choice, sister. You have given me *time. Time* to remember…"

"I like that you call me sister."

Haana smiled. "I have one more truth to share, Skeetu. Sticklegs have *two* legs. One whisperflute for each of us. You have oldkin to play for. I have sahaar to play for—Rin… Mother, Father, little Momo… When we find the sticklegs, well… maybe I will come back here. We will *both* come back here. Soohla will be glad to see us. She will have grown fat on buffalo meat and brush hens."

"She won't come looking for us?"

"No. She seemed very happy there. We will be, too."

"Where do we go now?" asked Skeetu.

"To find a turtle bog," said Haana.

Chapter 25

Skeetu and Haana searched the land for two months. Finding a turtle bog in the cold season, when the turtles slept in the muddy bottoms, was a great challenge. Once, Skeetu spotted what she believed to be a line of sticklegs, flying south high in the air. They raced in that direction, but lost sight of them.

"Now we know they are real," said Haana.

"We knew," said Skeetu. "Or we wouldn't be here."

The winter stretched on, longer than the one that came before. Haana had shown the oldkin how the sahaar shaped their hides to their limbs, using a bone needle to pull threads through the skins. Skeetu was grateful for the extra warmth the snugger fitting mammoth hide provided. She had also grown as adept as any sahaar at starting fires with the sparking stones.

"Uncle said that some oldkin from long ago could do this. I did not believe him. But he said it was true and that when he went to the lights in the sky, he brought the secret with him."

"It was the rocks," said Haana. "He could not have brought them with him."

"I know, but Uncle believed it was not the rocks, but him."

"It was the rocks," repeated Haana.

"I know."

Every day Skeetu practiced throwing her spear. She had long ago grown more deadly with it from a distance than Haana. She knew it was because of Rin's feather. One morning, while hunting the edge of a frozen marsh, a silent warning washed through her. Behind her stalked a clawtooth. It was very young, though, probably on one of its first hunts away from its mother. Skeetu raised her spear to take it down. The clawtooth stopped its approach. It let out a yell, squeaky and broken, and every bit the opposite of frightening. The girl lowered her spear and laughed.

"I may be sorry one day," she said, "But I cannot take your life." She lunged at the cat to scare it off. It spun and disappeared into the brush. Suddenly, Bulo came charging through, chasing after it. Skeetu was about to try and stop him, but knew he'd never come close to catching a racing clawtooth. *And maybe that will make it think again about following me.*

***

One night, the oldkin and sahaar sat at the fire, each traveling in their thoughts. They had pulled some plants from a turtlebog they camped at and cooked the roots on coals near the base of the flames.

"I am starting to forget things I did not want to," said Haana.

"What are you forgetting?"

"Others. Mother. Father."

"Rin?"

"No, but I remember him less."

"Is that good?"

"I do not know. It is frightening, though."

Skeetu thought a moment. "I can bring him back, a little," she said.

Haana looked up from the fire. "How?"

"Would you like to hear his song now?"

"Yes, Skeetu! I had… forgotten. Yes!"

The oldkin took out her flute and played the song of Rin. Haana listened with her eyes closed; swaying, smiling. It went on for some time, Skeetu following the music where it led her.

When it was over, Haana said, "There he is. Thank you, sister."

In the morning, they gathered their things to set out to find another bog. They had waited here for three days. Skeetu thought this one would have been a good possibility because the water was unfrozen in its center. Bulo was ready to move on, anyway. There was not much here he was interested in eating. The two decided to head to the crest of a hill about a day's hike away. From there, they should be able to see what was around them. They arrived in the night and were too tired to build a fire. Tonight, would be spent, as many previous, tucked up against the warmth of their gentle spearnose.

"Do you wonder how Soohla is doing?" asked Haana.

"I do."

"Me, too. I miss her."

"I do, too," said Skeetu.

"I think she is happy."

"I do, too."

"I think a lot about what it is like there," said Haana. "I miss the sahaar. I feel I should be with them. I feel them pulling me." Skeetu said nothing. *She has been missing them more and more. Soon it will just be Skeetu and Bulo, again.*

Then Haana quickly turned to the oldkin. "You are still my sister," she said. "You will always be. You are just not many, and I miss the many. Don't you?"

"Sometimes," she answered. "Not as much as I used to."

"But you, *we*, have been searching for the way for you to find them. You *must* miss them!"

"I do. But now I would be happy to just say goodbye. It is why I chase this sticklegs. Just to say goodbye. That cave bear took that from me. I will take it back."

"And then?"

"I don't know. Do you hear that?"

The two looked up. A flock of birds flew overhead, honking and cackling. The girls stood and watched their silhouettes drop down out of sight just beyond the next hill.

"Is that…" began Haana.

"I think they are!" said Skeetu.

"How far?"

"Half a day? Do we go now?"

"No, but we will go at first light."

"I am going now," said the oldkin.

"I won't be able to keep up but go ahead. I will follow your trail."

"No," said Skeetu. "There are clawtooths here. We will stay together."

"First light. I promise."

***

Skeetu slept very little that night. They were too close to stop. But she couldn't leave Haana on her own. The sahaar had no problem sleeping. The last push up the hill was difficult. Sometimes Skeetu forgot that her oldkin legs were stronger than those of her friend.

The moon had dropped below the trees. First light would be rising soon. Skeetu could wait no longer. She shook Haana awake.

"Let's go," she said.

"It's dark," said Haana.

"Let's go."

They climbed down the hill, pushed through the valley and worked their way up the next hill. From the

185

direction they headed, it appeared the birds landed on the other side. When they reached the top, they scanned the area. Countless small bodies of water dotted the landscape. A large one off to the south had movement in it, tiny pale dots. Skeetu squinted. She turned and looked at Haana, who was straining to see in the distance.

"Haana?"

The girl turned her head to the oldkin. She read Skeetu's face. "Is it? Are they?"

Skeetu grabbed her shoulders. *"Yes! Sticklegs!"*

Haana returned her gaze to the lakes. "Are all of those moving things them?"

"Long beak, a longer neck, and even longer legs made from the branches of a puff willow, yes?"

"Yes!" said Haana. "Red heads? Do they have red heads like Chup said?"

"Too far to tell. But it is them, Haana! We found them!"

"What do we do?"

"We have to get closer, but we need to be careful not to scare them off."

"What about Bulo?"

Skeetu forgot about him. The rhino was awake and had wandered off.

"We'll find him later. Water birds aren't afraid of him, though. I think they know which animals hunt them and which ones do not."

They raced down the hill and slowed when they reached the tall reeds that surrounded the lake.

"This isn't a turtlebog," whispered Haana.

"Shh, don't tell the sticklegs," said Skeetu. Haana giggled.

They came to a place where they could peek through the vegetation and into the open water.

And there they were.

Skeetu thought there were more than needles on a needletree. Their noise vibrated in her ears. They sounded like squeaky flutes filled with loose gravel. The oldkin stared, transfixed at the sight and the sounds of these graceful creatures. While she had known she would find one someday, she could never actually imagine what it would feel like to stand among them. She had always stalked the birds, learned their songs and sang them back to them. They drew her to them. This was something different. The sahaar talked about something called spirits. They once thought *she* was one. And Bulo. *Bodies that had no real body and flew like birds.* They were from another place where other creatures lived. If such things were real, then they lived among the sticklegs. The oldkin could feel it. She now saw why Chup said it would be wrong to take one's life. This brought to mind a problem.

"Haana," she whispered. "How do we find one that is dying?"

"Oh," said the girl. She, too, had been mesmerized by the sight of the endless flock of birds. "I don't know."

"We always worried about finding them, but never what we would do when we did."

The sahaar was silent. So was Skeetu. She scanned the flock as they waded through the shallow lake. The water was up to the birds' knees, knees black and knobby like the branches of the puff willow. Every so often there was a gentle 'blip' as one pulled a meal from the mud with its long beak. The oldkin saw the red on top of the heads Chup spoke of, as if each were attacked by an oldkin trying to take her flute back. If any were sick, she couldn't tell. Now she was afraid that after finally finding them, they would all take off, leaving her back where she started.

A spear flew through the air. It had come from behind her. She watched it arc up and then drop down. Everything moved slowly through the oldkin's eyes. The sounds of the birds slowed as well, growing deeper and drawn out. The spear appeared to be floating, then dropping, slowly, slowly… It struck one of the birds in the flank. It sputtered around in the water. The birds around it took off in a massive 'whoosh' of wings. They were gone. Skeetu turned and looked at Haana.

"What did you do?"

The sahaar smiled.

Chapter 26

"Why did you do that?" demanded the oldkin.

"So you could be with it as it left our land," said her friend. "Go to the bird."

Skeetu stared at her friend. She didn't know what to say. "Come with me."

They ran to the sticklegs. It was still breathing, but its eyes were closed. Skeetu pulled the spear from its thigh and sat in the mud. She rested the bird's limp head on her lap.

"Why?" she asked again.

"This was what you wanted," answered Haana.

"No! It cannot happen this way! Chup said that the bird must not be killed."

"He said *you* must not kill it. You did not kill it. I did," said the sahaar. "For you. For my sister who is alone in the land."

"But…"

"I don't want the whisperflute any more, Skeetu. I don't want to live for what is gone. For *who* is gone. I am ready to return to be with my sahaar, as Soohla has done. You gave me that time—that gift. And I gave you this gift."

"You are going back?"

"Yes, but can I ask one thing from you?"

"Yes, Haana. Always."

"Will you return with me? If I cannot convince you to join us, then you can leave at the hill above their valley."

"I will do this. But I will not go with you to the sahaar."

"I will try to change your mind."

"I know… Would you leave me now? I feel the bird's breathing is changing. I want to ease its way home."

Haana walked away. She came upon Bulo who had followed their trail and shoved against his massive bulk to turn him around. The spearnose knew what that meant and splashed away from the edge of the lake with the girl.

Skeetu looked down at the bird Haana had speared.

"I am sorry for this," she said, softly. A tear dropped onto the feathered black cheek of the bird, as she truly was saddened by what had been done. The oldkin had taken the lives of many animals. It was how one lived. Many animals take the lives of many animals. It was not wrong. It was not right. It just was. This did not feel the same. This was not for food. She tried to convince herself that the bird's song would now be sung for the family it had lost. *But it did not ask for this. It may not care. It may have wished to stay with the other sticklegs, flying beneath the moon, catching crawlers in the mud…*

Skeetu sang for the dying bird. She used no words, which it would not understand, but hummed soft notes she hoped would ease its worries. The song was not for the promise of the whisperflute she would make of its leg. It was for the life of the bird itself, a thing that meant everything to it, but was now nearly gone.

And then it was.

Skeetu stepped out from the reeds and walked to Haana and Bulo, who waited for her in muddy snow. Haana was stroking the spearnose's neck to keep him from wandering to find his oldkin.

"Do you have them?" asked the sahaar. Skeetu held up her pouch in response.

"Are you okay?"

"No," said the oldkin. "This does not feel right for the bird."

"I'm sorry," said the girl. She was silent a moment, and then said, "They will have to dry a while before you can carve them."

"Okay. This did not make me happy, Haana."

"I don't think it should have. I don't think it would work if you found joy in this."

"No."

"Should I show you how to make the flute?"

"No. I will do it. After I see you to your sahaar, I am returning to Father's hill. I will play the flute there."

"You would go all the way back?"

"Bulo and I have made the journey before. I have no oldkin like you have sahaar, but I still have a place where they once were. I want to be there."

***

It took them a full pass of the moon to reach the plains beneath the scrubhills. It hadn't snowed in a while and the wind had cleared out large swaths of exposed land. Bulo, who was still bulging from when they last visited the area, set back to work clearing the ground of leafy plants.

"I don't think he will be able to walk back with you," joked Haana.

Skeetu laughed. She watched her spearnose with a smile on her face.

"I am glad you have him with you, Skeetu."

"I am, too."

"I think he will be loved by the sahaar over that hill. Yes?"

The oldkin laughed again. "Yes. He would feed them for days."

"Oh no. Not Bulo. Come with me, Skeetu. You should not be alone. You are my sister and I do not ever want to forget you."

"You would forget *us*?"

"I forget everything. But I would not if I saw you every day."

192

Skeetu reached into her pouch and pulled out the flute Haana had given her. So much had happened since that day at her valley. "Take this back. If you start to forget me, play it."

"You said when I do it makes your ears hurt," said the sahaar.

"Then remember that, too, and play better!"

Haana took the flute. Then she hugged her friend.

"Goodbye, sister."

"Goodbye, sister. Know that I will always remember *you*. And your brother Rin will live inside me, too. Always."

Haana smiled. She gave Bulo's chin a gentle scratch and then looked back at Skeetu. The girl opened her mouth, as if to try and convince her one more time to come with her but seemed to realize it was useless.

Skeetu watched her as she walked away. She was afraid for her, afraid that maybe the new sahaar were not what they seemed. But it was what Haana wanted, enough to take that risk. *She is very brave*, thought her friend. The girl disappeared over the hill. Skeetu caught up with Bulo.

"Come," she said. "We are going home."

The two left the scrubhills and headed back north to Skeetu's land. They went the same way they came, though their trail was nearly wiped clean by the wind. Bulo knew where he was going. He always seemed to know where he was going.

***

One night, as she sat at the fire, she pulled out the two leg bones. They were black as the charred sticks at the edge of the flames. When she held them in her hand, though, they didn't feel… *special.* They were simply two leg bones. *Was Chup wrong?* She had to believe he spoke the truth, or at least what he believed it to be. And then she remembered what she had felt when she saw the flock on the lake. *He was not wrong.* The oldkin cut them down to shorter lengths, to about that of her arm between her wrist and elbow. They would be easier to carry without breaking them. She would wait until they dried a bit more before carving them, a thing she feared greatly. Her biggest concern at first was finding the bird. That concern was then replaced with finding one that was dying. She always knew, though, what she should have feared most was that she could not make the flute. She had not been able to do that in the past. Why would it be different now?

Then she heard the snap of a branch. Skeetu stood and searched around her. After staring so long into the flames, she was blind in the darkness. *The wolf?* The oldkin slapped the sleeping spearnose on his flank.

"Up, Bulo." The rhino quickly climbed to his feet. He knew the fear in his oldkin's voice. Skeetu held her spear and circled around the fire. She didn't want to wander too far from it, as it kept away certain large oldkin-eating beasts.

"Hoo, hoo!" she called out.

"Skeetu?" called a voice.

"Haana? Haana, you followed me!"

But it wasn't Haana. A girl stepped into the light of the flames.

"Dami?"

Chapter 27

"Look at this, Dugg! Isn't it beautiful?" Jen held the shell out to her dog, and then brought it back up to her face. "The carvings are… exquisite!" They were clearly etched with a fine, sharp stone, and formed a circular, wavy pattern with a dot in the middle. Lines, like rays of the sun, emanated from the center. It was obvious by the two holes in its sides that it was meant to be worn, likely around the neck. *This was one special Neanderthal,* she thought. *The Leonardo DaVinci of her time! She plays music… makes jewelry…*

Many of her colleagues believed that *neanderthalensis* did create art, and there was some evidence to back this up. But no evidence as strong as finding, first a flute, and then a carved shell in one's possession. The only thing dampening her spirits was that back at home she was a wanted woman. A fugitive. Which was no small thing…

That, and she *was* stranded in the desert. For some reason that concerned her less than her legal problems. For now, though, there was nothing she could do about either dilemma. After a lifetime of planning out what she'd be doing next, she was now living in the moment. There was a certain freedom to that. She put the shell aside and retrieved the flute from Neandergirl's 'bed'. It was almost freed from its blockage. Jen crawled back under the tarp and chipped away. Then at last, in the glowing orange of the setting sun, she broke through. She held the flute to her mouth and blew, clearing out the loosened debris. She looked through the mouthpiece at the sun. *Almost there. Will I finally get to hear it?*

She dug out her stiff bottlebrush and plunged the hole until it was smooth inside. It was finished. Or so she hoped. Jen had never played this kind of instrument before. The closest she had come was playing the recorder in third grade. And she hadn't been very good at that. She blew through the mouthpiece. Nothing. Just air through a tube. *It must be like playing a bottle.* She tipped it a little and blew across the opening. Still nothing.

"Ugh! It doesn't work!" After all this, at the very end it was for nothing. *Keep trying.* She held it in a few different positions against her lips and finally found a note. With that note came an explosion of images! She pulled it away, alarmed. She was breathing quickly, making herself dizzy. Then she gave it another blow. It made a sound, and again images of people—women— filled her head. In that one breath, dozens of faces flew past her, whizzing by as if she were watching a film in fast-forward. She felt as if she knew these people, but she didn't have the time to linger and get to know them better. While their images were fleeting, she could see they were dressed in simple clothes. Some were peasants. Some were slightly better off. She played some more as history flew backwards. She wondered how far it would take her. *To the one who made this, I would think... to Neandergirl?*

Jen played for hours. She got a little better at it and was actually finding notes that were not entirely unpleasant. The clearer the note, she discovered, the clearer the memory of the people passing through at that moment, so she focused on that, on the quality of the tone. She played up into what she believed to be the Bronze Age, somewhere in Europe. Maybe Great Britain? She felt that if she could play better, it would be easier to track her advance, or retreat, actually. That would have to be all for the night, though. The constant exhalation needed to play the instrument had made her quite lightheaded. *Circular breathing,* she thought. She heard that's what horn players did but wasn't really sure what that meant.

Jen stood and placed the flute back in Neandergirl's spot. She laid a towel over it for protection but wasn't exactly sure what that would protect it from. Dugg, probably.

Tomorrow I will get to the beginning. The reason for this all, she thought. This was so much to take in. At last, she had reached the culmination of her journey. Would it have been worth all it cost her? She walked to the edge of site and looked up at the star-packed sky. Out here it seemed there were more stars than there was space between them. Neandergirl must have looked up that those stars. What did she think of when she did?

A lizard darted across her bare foot, and she jumped. The archeologist lost her footing and slid over the edge. It was a steep drop for about eight feet, and she went down headfirst. Her body flipped again, and she landed hard on her ankle with a loud, nauseating crack. Jen screamed in pain at the top of her lungs. She fell onto her back and laid still, afraid to look at what she'd done to herself. This was worse than the scorpion bite—much worse! And it was the same stupid ankle! She worked her hands down her leg, putting off for as long as she could feeling for a broken bone in her leg below her shin, which is what she expected. When she got there, it was what she found.

"*Nooooo*" she screamed until she was hoarse. More than the pain was the realization that she was not only stranded in the desert, but stranded and unable to move. She felt like some hapless character in some dumb movie where every stupid thing that could happen to her did. *And every one of those stupid things was my own stupid fault!*

She heard a tinkling of metal off to the side. A dog collar. *Dugg!*

"Oh, Dugg! Look at me! What have I done to us?" The dog wagged his tail and licked her face. He sensed her despair, which made him nervous. Jen noticed the bandana around his neck and untied it. She wrapped it as best she could around her ankle, hoping to stabilize the bone. She passed out from the pain and woke to that ceiling of stars above. Jen rolled over and started to crawl up the hill to where her sleeping bag was. And her tarp. And water. *And the flute...* The sand was too loose, and she made no headway.

"Stay down here with me tonight, Dugg. We'll figure out how to get up there tomorrow." But what if she couldn't? She had just filled Dugg's water dish, but that wouldn't last very long. Even if he did not drink it, it would be evaporated by midafternoon. She had no choice. She was going to get up there. But tomorrow morning.

"It's going to be a cold night, boy," she said, pulling her dog to her. She hugged him tightly for his warmth, but also because he was the one thing in this world that brought her nothing but good.

Chapter 28

"Where's Rin?" asked Skeetu, shocked to see this sahaar girl before her. For a moment, she wondered if this was one of those spirits they spoke of, but no. It was Dami.

"Hello, Skeetu," said Dami, icily.

"Oh, I am sorry, Dami. We thought… are you all right? What happened?"

"We were following your spearnose's trail and I fell through a hole in the snow. Rin tried to grab me, but he fell, too."

"Is he… Did he…?"

"I don't know. I never saw him again! I tried to find him. For a long time, I tried!" Skeetu wanted to reach out to comfort her, but it was Dami, and she didn't like to be touched… by oldkin.

"I went back and saw that cliff. I did not think anyone could survive that fall!"

"The snow was deep at the bottom. I was buried for two days, I think. I thought I would never pull myself free. But I had this," she said, tapping the shell hanging against her chest. "Where are the others? Haana and Soohla?"

"With the new sahaar. It is about three days from here. Two nights, three days."

"They are friendly?"

"That is what they said. I hope so."

"You will take me there?"

Skeetu laughed. "No! I just came from there. I will tell you how to find it."

"Okay," said the girl. She looked at the feather hanging from the oldkin's spear and frowned. "Does it fly like a bird now?"

"It does. Why did it take you so long to find your way back, Dami?"

"I searched for Rin. And then I got lost—very lost. I had my own sparking stones for fire, and I tunneled into the snow at night to stay warm. It was still very cold…" Dami laughed to herself. "It was lucky I did not lose the batbear meat."

"Did you like it?"

"At first, no. But it tasted better as it ran out. Haana was right. I never lost my spear, so I was able to find more food—enough to keep me alive."

"Are you hungry?"

"Yes." Skeetu shared some of the ground pig she had put aside for tomorrow. There would be more when she needed it. Dami ate hungrily. When she was done, she licked her fingers and then rubbed them clean in the snow, as she'd always done. The oldkin had never seen one so concerned with keeping her hands clean.

Skeetu filled the sahaar in on what had happened since she was separated from the others. The girl listened in silence as she stared into the flames. When she finished, Dami asked her about the whisperflute bones.

"You are going to make the flute yourself?"

"Yes, Dami. I know you think oldkin are not able to do anything."

"That is not true."

"I know."

"No, it is not true that I think that. Skeetu, I am going to tell you something I have told no one. I think it is safe because you will not be able to tell this to the other sahaar. You are not going to stay with them, no?"

"No."

"My mother was oldkin."

"How… What… what are you saying?"

"Father told me a long time ago. He said to tell no one because he was afraid the sahaar in the valley would not take us in."

"She was oldkin?" This was hard to believe. Skeetu did not know that oldkin and sahaar could make children. But when she looked at the girl, the light of the fire awoke the faint tints of red in her hair. Like the lichen on the rocks by the lake. She had only known the sahaar to have black hair.

"Yes. Father said he lived with a small clan of oldkin. Like your own. They took him in when he was younger. He said he had no memory of what happened to his family. *They* became his family."

"Why did he leave them?"

"He would not say. But he did say some of them made things hard for him. He did not say how. He took me from my mother and looked for sahaar."

"Do you know where the oldkin are? Where they were?"

"No."

This shattered Skeetu's hope of finding more of her own. *But Dami is one of my own now. She always was.*

"If you ever see the others again, you must not tell them this," said the girl.

"I don't think I will see them, Dami. But I don't think they would care. They call me sister. They would still call you sister."

"Maybe." Dami lied down and wriggled closer to the fire, with her back to Skeetu. "I am tired," she said, and went to sleep.

***

In the morning, Skeetu took the girl to the top of a hill and pointed to where her friends had gone. Considering the journey she had undertaken to find her way back here, what lay ahead would be easy for her. *I am surprised that I am sad to see her go. More, now that I know where she came from. Are we the last two oldkin in the land?*

"Are you sure you want to go there?" she asked her.

"Yes," said Dami. "Are you sure you do not?"

"Yes."

"I am a little afraid, though."

"You should be," said Skeetu. Then she thought better of what she said. *Now I sound like Dami.* "You will be all right. Tell Soohla I smile when I think of her falling out of trees. And tell Haana, I remember everything."

"I will."

"Dami, do you think Rin could still be alive?"

A sudden sadness appeared on her face. She looked down at the snow. "I don't think so. But *I* was. So I thought he could be. I really tried to find him, Skeetu! He was… he was my favorite of everyone. I always…"

"I know," said the oldkin. "We all did. Maybe one day he will just appear in the new valley. And your heart will go…" Skeetu tapped her chest rapidly.

"Maybe." Dami removed the shell from around her neck and handed it to Skeetu. "Take this."

"This is your luck shell! I cannot take it!"

"I want you to have it, Skeetu. I have not always been kind to you, but I am here because of you."

"Will it work for me?"

"Ha! We are oldkin! If it worked for me, it will for you. I would not be alive without it. But now that you have shown me where I need to go, I no longer need one. And if I do, *psshhh…* I will just make another."

Skeetu held the shell in her hands. She was always drawn to the image scratched on its surface—circles with lines radiating out from the center. It felt like it existed between two places; where she stood now, and another place where she walked in her dreams—almost like when she was on Father's hill.

"Thank you," was all she could think to say.

The oldkin stood and watched Dami disappear over the crest of the hill, just as she had done days before with Haana. Her hand rested on the shell hanging from her neck, but it was not the girl who made it she thought of.

Chapter 29

Skeetu and Bulo made their way back to Father's hill. They still had a journey ahead, but she was grateful the weather had not made things more difficult. In fact, today was unusually mild and the snow melting from the tree branches sounded like falling rain. It made her impatient for the warm season on its way. The oldkin was able to shed the heavy mammoth skins and enjoy the feel of the air on her own.

Skeetu set the stickleg bones out on a flat rock and began the work on one of them. She carved a stick with a sharp stone and used it to drill out the inside. This was the easy part, as the bone meat was still soft. Then she trimmed down the length at both ends and went to work on the holes. First, she closed her eyes and tried to picture the flute she had given back to Haana. *I should have kept it so I could copy it,* she thought. *No. I am happy she has it.*

Bulo wandered up and made her jump. He was growing restless to leave.

"How did I not hear you?" She gave his leg a scratch and then patted him away. "Go, go, go. I have to do this now, Bulo. We will go later."

Skeetu had already prepared a thinly pointed stone for making the holes. There would be four, each a slightly different size, which is how Haana always made them. *Here we go...* She twisted the stone into the bone, and it cut through easily. After making three holes, she held it up to inspect her work. Something was a little off. It was close to the image in her head, but it was not the same. *Maybe with the last hole it will look right.* She pressed the drill into the bone and heard a crack. The oldkin held her breath and pulled her hands away, dropping the drill. She bent forward for a closer look. The bone had split all the way up its length.

"*What did I do?*" she shouted. "What did I do?" Bulo came up to her again, but she pushed him back. "Go! Not now!"

Gently, Skeetu picked up the flute. *I can wrap it with grass to hold it together. But will it work the same? Will the stickleg spirit fly with me through a broken bone?* Then without thinking, she smashed it into the rock. The oldkin beat the cracked flute with her fist. Maddened with anger and frustration, she turned the bone to a pile of black chips. Then she looked over to the one next to it. She was breathing heavily, and her hands shook with rage. She was about to crush the second one but managed to gain control of herself. If Haana had not given her two chances at making a whisperflute... She knew this would happen!

Skeetu wrapped the remaining bone and placed it back in her pouch. She would attempt this one tomorrow. The first one was a lesson. She could not make any more mistakes.

***

The oldkin and spearnose traveled another day. They arrived at the base of the cave ledge where they'd been attacked by the batbears. She decided to go a different way. They trod around the bottom of the ridge, instead of climbing up and pushing across, which was the way they came. The batbears were certainly a concern, but she also did not want to see what she knew would be left of Chup inside the cave. The thought of it brought back memories of the day she lost her family. If Chup were alive, she would smell the smoke from his fire, even from here. *Maybe he left, and made it to join the others.* It was a good thought to hold on to.

They reached an open area where she could see, in all directions, if any dangerous beasts were coming for her. It was another warm day and she decided it was time for her last attempt at making the flute. As she had done the day before, she laid it out on a flat rock, along with her tools. Although this time, it was frighteningly obvious she had no back up sitting next to it. Skeetu hollowed it out, trimmed the ends and prepared to drill the holes. This was always where she went wrong. She closed her eyes and tried to envision Haana's flute. The length was right. The holes… *Wait!* She noticed something she had never seen before. She stayed with that image longer—studied it more closely. She pored over every tiny detail in her memory. Carefully, and holding her breath, she drilled the first hole. Before she drilled the second one, she made a small mark where it would go. She had never done that before, but she could see now that it helped her plan what she would do before she did it. The picture in her head, of Haana's flute, showed her what she had always done wrong. The holes needed to line up straight. And with an equal distance between each one. Hers were always… off center, a little more randomly placed. She held her breath and drilled the second hole and quickly pulled the stone away before she went too far. The oldkin released her breath and steadied herself for the third hole. Her hands were shaking, and she waited until they grew steady again. She drilled the third hole, and again, quickly pulled her hands away. *One left…*

"I don't want to do this," she said. "Maybe three is enough?" *No,* she thought. It was not how the sahaar had made them. Why would an oldkin know better?

She made a mark where the last hole would go. It lined up straight with the other three. She set the tip of the stone on the bone and twisted it between her fingers. The drill bit into it and punctured through, into the hollow tube. Skeetu stopped. She pulled out the stone tip and set it aside, far from the flute, should it somehow grow a desire to leap upon it and cut through some more.

"I think I did it," she whispered. "I think I did it." The oldkin was covered in sweat and out of breath, as if she had run up the side of a mountain. She was more than a little dizzy. But at that moment in time, she felt that she had done the most difficult thing in her life. And, maybe, the most important. The girl was afraid to pick up the flute, lest she drop it, so she just leaned forward and stared at it for a good long time.

A strong breeze picked up, rolling the instrument across the rock and Skeetu snatched it up and cradled it to her chest. The image of her mother drifted through her, that breeze her soft breath. She wrapped the flute in a hare skin and gently placed it in her pouch. The sky was turning gray. Another storm was coming. *Maybe tonight, surely by morning.* She found a shallow shelter in the side of the hill and collected wood for a fire. She was in batbear land and hoped the flames would keep them away. Bulo, thankfully, stayed nearby. *Does he remember this place? Of course he does!*

In the morning they would continue their push to Father's hill. She would not bring the whisperflute to her lips until she arrived. Everything had to be just right, and she could think of no better place to play for those she still missed so much. That she could ease their worries about her made her feel light inside. Skeetu looked up toward where she believed Chup's cave to be, the one with the unsettling drawings of hornbeards on the walls. *Thank you, Chup,* she thought. *Your sticklegs were real. I have a whisperflute now.* Then she thought of Dami. *I told you I could do it!* She touched the shell on her chest and, for a moment, wondered if Dami had helped her after all.

Things were looking like they were finally going to bring her to a place she wished to be. Her friends, most of them, were with their people. Rin was gone, but if Dami survived, maybe he did, too. *He could be with his sister right now!* That night, she slept more peacefully than she had in a very long time. She dreamed of her mother and wished to stay in that place for the rest of her days. She was awakened only once, by the howling of a wolf far, far away. Skeetu drifted easily back to sleep, as the sound brought to mind her cozy needletree forest home.

***

She awoke to a blizzard. Skeetu shivered in the wet, frigid air, the fire having long been snuffed by the snow. It was much like the storm that came upon them when she last passed through here, the one that drove them into Chup's cave. She shook Bulo awake, and they pushed through to make their way north.

It snowed for days and was still going strong when they finally were in sight of the needletree forest. Seeing the wall of green after nothing but white and grey lifted the gloom. The moon had come and gone and returned since she'd left Dami. Her journey was coming to an end. In another day they would be back to her shelter if it was still standing. She hoped it was. She needed rest.

Then it would be another day to Father's hill. And then… And then she would be a new Skeetu! Her past would have been washed away. She and Bulo would wander the land with nowhere to go. Maybe they would find more oldkin. Or she and her spearnose could haunt the edges of a sahaar camp, becoming once again spirits spoken of in frightened whispers. Skeetu could not move on to a new thing until she finished the old thing that drove her. It would soon be time to say goodbye to that old thing.

They plowed through the snow and reached the forest. Her shelter had collapsed, but that was okay. She could still burrow inside. Mice had chewed holes through what hides she had left behind, but that was okay, too. In the morning they would set out for the hill.

***

The snow stopped falling in the night and sunlight slipped in through the boughs of her shelter. Skeetu dug herself out and cleared an area to make a fire. She dried her skins, bundled up and headed into the great open area between the forest and river. Bulo followed closely behind her. The snow was too deep for him to forage for greens, so there was nothing to slow him down.

Then, in the distance, she saw a large, dark shape. *Mammoth? No… spearnose!* It was a huge male, considerably bigger than Bulo. Skeetu was worried it might attack her friend. It was far enough away that it

213

couldn't see them. Spearnoses didn't have the strongest eyesight. Maybe it would keep going. She turned and pulled down on Bulo's fur, trying to get him to lie down so he'd be hidden in the deep snow. He wasn't sure what she was doing at first but caught on. He dropped onto his belly. Skeetu brought her face to his ear so she could feed him a flow of quiet, comforting words.

"Stay here," she whispered. "We will just rest a little…" She hummed softly, as she did when she first comforted her friend, that night he lost his mother. *Could that be his father out there? Would he know his son? Would it matter if he did?*

Suddenly, Bulo began to shudder.

"Oh no." Skeetu knew what was coming. "Not now! Not now!" she whispered frantically. But she knew nothing would stop it.

The woolly rhino climbed to his feet and charged in circles around the oldkin, huffing and snorting, loudly. Skeetu watched the spearnose in the distance, hoping it would not notice them. But it did. It changed direction and charged toward them. Bulo was still wherever he went when the madness took him. He didn't see the rhino. He circled one more time and shook his head, bringing himself back to his normal state.

"*Look out!*" shouted Skeetu as the great spearnose crashed into her friend. Bulo was sent skidding across the snow.

"*Bulo!*"

The spearnose turned on her. The oldkin tried to run, but the snow was too deep. Its horn caught her mammoth hide and with a flick of its head, tossed her in the air. Skeetu landed hard, twenty feet away, her pouch, with her flute and Rin's sparking stones, several feet beyond that.

Bulo had climbed back to his feet and went after the other, much larger spearnose. They met head-to-head, the clacking of their horns sounding like two trees knocking together in a storm. Bulo tried to get his horn under the other, to catch it underneath, but the great spearnose pushed forward, easily sliding the smaller one back. They stood shoulder to shoulder, each dropping his head to drive its horns into the other's throat or belly. Bulo was flipped onto his back and struggled to get up.

Skeetu was unable to move. She couldn't breathe. There was a roaring in her ears, like the tumbling fastwater of the high rivers. The sound muted the deep grunts of the two beasts. She felt the rumble through the ground, but half buried in the snow, she was unable to see what was happening. She didn't want to see. The battle was taking place a good distance away now. Still fighting for air, with her back pressed against the ground, she could feel the pounding as if it were right beside her. And then she heard it. A long, drawn, gurgling groan. The ground shook one more time and then was still.

"Bulo," she tried to shout, but his name barely left her throat. The thumping returned, but then grew softer as it moved away. The oldkin struggled to her knees, made more difficult as her hands kept breaking through the surface, dropping her onto her face. Her vision was blurred through a mask of snow, but she saw the angry spearnose limping toward the woods. It darted side to side, still enraged and looking for her. Off to the side was the blood-soaked mass of fur she knew was her friend. Her protector… She ducked down into the drift so the other one wouldn't see her.

"Bulo," she said again. She began to cry, but it was still too hard to breath. *What just happened?* In one short moment everything she had was gone. Just a few breaths earlier, she was happy and hopeful for the days to come. *Just a few breaths! How could everything change in just a few breaths?*

Skeetu saw the corner of her pouch sticking out of the snow. Beyond that was her whisperflute, just barely poking up from the surface. The spearnose was gone. She pulled herself over to the flute, every inch sending a wave of pain through her body. She wasn't sure what was wrong with her, but her body wasn't working as it should. She got sick in the snow and saw blood. The oldkin grabbed the whisperflute and rolled onto her back. She could no longer move. Her hides were torn, and snow was packed around her bare, shivering skin. She knew she had to get to her feet, to keep moving, to stay warm, but she could not. She lay on her back, arms outstretched, the flute in her unfeeling hand. The night came. The pain had left her body. She now felt nothing.

Then the shivering stopped. Above, the lights of her ancestors blinked away. Each a spark from the great fire. Skeetu wished she could bring the flute to her lips to speak to them. The lights blurred. And then went dark.

Chapter 30

Jen shivered. It was morning. Dugg had stayed with her through the night, his warm body keeping her alive in the cold desert. Another sun was rising. Soon she would be wishing for the return of the cool of night.

"Water…" Her water jug was up the hill. So were the extra jugs. She wondered if she'd have better luck reaching them this morning. She looked at her ankle. It was terribly swollen and bent in an unnatural angle. Dugg returned from exploring the perimeter, wagging his tail.

"What have I done to us? I'm sorry, Dugg. You should have stayed home. We should have…"

Jen rolled onto her hands and knees. *I have to get up there!* It was a fifteen-foot climb to the ridge where the food and water was. Trying to keep her ankle off the ground, she began crawling up the side. She bit into her lip so hard to stop from screaming, her teeth drew blood. Her ankle was filled with broken pieces of glass, or so it felt. She'd make it two or three feet and then slide down again.

It's like an antlion trap, she thought, thinking of those insects that made pits in the sand to trap their prey. Jen tried for over an hour but accomplished nothing more than passing out from the pain. She rolled over and watched the sun float higher in the sky. It felt like it was glaring down at her, bent on torturing this sorry creature in the sand.

"Need water…" She would need shade, too, and eventually food, but without water, none of that would matter. *Up the hill. I will do it!* She got back onto her hands and knees and resumed her attempt to scale the hill. This time she was determined not to let the pain stop her. She kept her belly to the sand and inched upward. Jen could feel gravity pulling her back. She made it six feet and rolled down. Her body spun and whipped her foot onto the ground. She cried out. Dugg came to her side again.

"I can't do it, Dugg! I can't do it!"

The temperature rose quickly. Not a cloud floated above. Jen was wearing only a T-shirt and jeans. Her shoes were above, probably housing scorpions. She pulled the collar of the shirt up over her face to give it some protection from the burning orb pulsing down on her. The day was spent slipping in and out of dreams. Dreams of family. They were still coming from the flute that rested with Neandergirl's spirit above. But they were foggy and jumbled. The flute was so close but might as well have been a thousand miles away.

***

That night was spent in the same spot. The archeologist was severely dehydrated and was beginning to see things that weren't there. What would the next day bring? Would tomorrow be her last? If it was, she could accept it, but what had she done to her dog? He played no role in this bizarre, unfair… utterly ridiculous end. Just months ago, she was exploring this desert with her colleagues, excited by possibilities. And now…

"How did I get here?" she muttered, and hugged Dugg closer as the cold crept in.

***

She survived the night. Dugg was gone again. She tried to whistle for him, but her lips were cracked. *Water…* Jen shifted her position in the sand, the simple act bringing on more exhaustion. Every movement was a struggle. Her ankle no longer hurt, though. She thought that was probably not good.

The afternoon sun was as punishing as it had been the day before. Oddly, her skin felt cool and dry. *Heat stroke… there you are…* A warm breath pulsed in her right ear. She turned her head. *Dugg. Breathing. Flute in mouth…*

Jen forced her eyes open. *Flute?* Her dog sat beside her. He was panting but tucked in the back of his mouth was the flute, once again.

"Dugg? Can… I have that please?" she asked, her voice dry as sand. Dugg dropped it and lay down beside her. Jen reached over with trembling hands and picked it up. With her last reserve of strength, she propped her back against the base of the hill. She brought the flute to her cracked lips and blew. She could only manage short bursts, but it was enough. The faces returned. Their lives, generation after generation, crammed into mere seconds. Bronze Age to Neolithic to Mesolithic to Paleolithic. The further back she went, the faster time flew by. *Stone Age. I'm there.*

And then she saw her. It was the girl who made the flute. Neandergirl. *Skeetu? Her name is Skeetu!* She gazed at her pale face, thick, dark red hair, and the most deep, open… *honest* brown eyes she had ever seen. Honest was truly the word that came to mind. *Nothing hidden behind or within.* They offered a vision of the world unmarred by generations of the fears and sins of modern times.

Skeetu?

The girl looked toward her. Jen's dreams were always a two-way street. She would be that person, but also observed from the outside. And as Skeetu, she could talk to herself.

Yes? asked the girl.

Hi. I'm Jen.

We are dreaming now?

Yes. I found something that belongs to you.

My flute?

Yes. You did a good job making it.

It was hard. I broke the first one.

You made this to comfort your family, yes?

Yes.

You are a good person.

Are you oldkin?

A little tiny bit, Skeetu. You are family.

How?

I'm not really sure. But I live in a time very, very far from yours. I am… sahaar? We all are now. But many are a little oldkin, too. Like Dami.

You know Dami?

I know what you know, Skeetu. I hope that doesn't frighten you.

No, said the oldkin. *This is a good dream.*

I have been looking for you.

Why?

I don't really know.

Am I dying? asked Skeetu.

Jen reached deeper into the oldkin's essence. Yes, she said. I am sorry. I think I am, too.

I am sorry, too.

You have done a lot, Skeetu. I see your life. Can you see mine?

Skeetu reached out with her thoughts. She saw nothing of Jen. She could only hear her voice.

No, she said.

I am sorry about Bulo, said Jen. I found him here, in this time, with you. Be happy that you have been together for so many lifetimes. I found your shell, too.

It didn't work.

I don't know. Maybe it helped you make this flute.

Maybe. Where are you?

In a desert—a hot place. It is cold there, now, yes?

Very, said Skeetu. *But I can't feel it any more. It is hot there?*

Very, said Jen.

I miss being warm.

The two were silent a moment.

I am tired, Jen.

Okay. I was very happy to meet you, Skeetu.

Okay. What is that noise?

Jen heard a high-pitched squeak. She opened her eyes. Dugg was sitting up and staring at the flute. He was whining, as he always did when he heard a siren go by, or any high-pitched sound. Jen mouthed 'sorry' to the dog. Her voice had left her. She brought the flute back to her lips and tried to blow but didn't have any air left in her. She dropped her hands to the sand and pulled in another breath of dry air. *Sorry,* she thought to her dog.

Something was thumping. She felt it beneath her, faint at first, but growing louder. Now she felt it in her chest, and then heard it.

'Thup-thup-thup-thup-thup…'

She opened her eyes. *Helicopter?*

Chapter 31

The wolf howled again. Skeetu's eyes flashed open. She turned her head but could not see above the snow that enveloped her. He sounded very close. Off to the side, much nearer to her ear, came a high-pitched whistle. *The whisperflute!* It was playing on its own! The sound was sharp, and wobbly. Whoever was playing it was worse than Haana! It made the wolf howl again. Then she remembered her dream. A sahaar from a warm place, far away. She had found her flute and played it to comfort someone from her past. *Me!* But here it was right now, in her hand! It had called the wolf. Who woke her.

Then all went quiet, first the whistling, and then the howling. Skeetu found the strength to prop herself up on her elbow to peer across the top of the snow. The wolf was just one leap away. It stared at the girl through curious, amber eyes. They were different, softer than the eyes of the clawtooth, which saw her only as a meal to take. The wolf seemed to be trying to understand why they were both there, face to face. It was as confused by this as she. Skeetu struggled to her knees. This may not be a cold, killing clawtooth, but it was still a wolf and wolves ate oldkins. Suddenly, it spun around and bounded away across the open plain.

Skeetu's body was still numb from the cold. The wolf may have woken her from her last sleep, but it was just putting off what was to come. If she could make it back to the forest… build a fire… but it was too far to go on dead, frozen limbs, through thigh-high, crusted-over snow. Her head fell forward as she drifted back off into the quiet place, and then jerked back up.

What is that? She felt a dull thump in the ground. And then another. They grew louder, and closer together.

'Thump… thump… *thump…thump*!'

Skeetu turned her head back to the forest. The spearnose had spotted her and was charging. Inside her mind, she reached for her spear to fight the beast off, but her body remained slumped in the snow, unmoving. *Wait…*

"Bulo?" She turned to look back at the dead spearnose in the distance. *That's not him.*

As Bulo ran toward her, she saw a dark shape emerge from the trees behind him. *Sahaar.* A male, young, tall, holding a spear with one red feather…

Epilogue

"Hello?" It was Hirnhoff. "Jen?"

"Yes?"

Why would he be calling? He had been the one to send the helicopter looking for her in the desert.

"How did you know?" Jen had asked when he called her in the hospital in Madrid.

"It was one of those things. When I realized you took off, I checked on our skeleton to see if you had stolen anything else from it. Sorry, but can you blame me? Then I got this feeling in my gut something was wrong. It made me call the local police garrison in the town by our dig. They said someone reported headlights deep in the desert that mysteriously disappeared. Figured, 'Who else would that be?'."

"And I had tried so hard not to be seen by that car! I'm thankful you trusted your gut. I thought you didn't believe in that kind of stuff."

"I don't. But I knew you were going back there. And I knew you weren't in your right mind. That gut feeling was the logical culmination of a progression of actions and delusions on your part. And it was too strong to ignore. I felt an urgency. Probably didn't hurt I was staring at a corpse when it hit me."

"A lot of science words for a gut feeling," said Jen.

"You owe the museum $15,380 for that ride."

"Can I have my job back, then?"

"Of course not."

He had never intended to press charges for stealing the flute and would keep her crime to himself until she chose to return it on her own, which, he said, he knew she would do. She was still fired, though. She wasn't sure if Hirnhoff was serious about her paying back the museum, but she suspected he was. And she would, somehow.

Her ankle was mostly healed, but she still used a cane on some days. None of this mattered to her much. Not an hour in the day went by that she did not revel in what she'd experienced. She had brought to life a dream chased by humans since their very existence.

I traveled through time.

Jen did return the flute, not that she had much choice. She was nearly unconscious when they found her. Dugg was fine, though. He had years of spoiling ahead of him.

And then there was this phone call out of the blue.

"Yes?" she repeated.

"Jen, are you… did you do something to it?" asked Dr Hirnhoff.

"What's *it*, Stan?"

"The body. The skull. The *neanderthalensis*. What's going on?"

"I don't know what you mean. I'm serious. What happened?" There was silence on the other end. "Stan?"

"Jen, when did you last look at that artifact?"

"I don't know. A year ago? Shortly after we brought it back?"

"And what would you say its age was?"

"*Her* age? Late teens. We never really got to dive into it, *on this end*, but that was my guess. Yours, too. Of course it turns out we were right, but you don't like me to talk about that. Why?"

"Well… I had another look at it this morning. I was actually considering bringing you back in on this. Fresh start, and all… earning your helicopter ride… But… late teens, you say, right?"

"Yes, Stan. What's wrong? You sound… weird."

"Jen, when I lifted the lid off the box, I was looking at the remains of an old woman. A *neanderthalensis*, but… of an advanced age! Teeth worn. Arthritis. Old, healed injuries… It's not what we found in the desert! But it's exactly the same body parts. Something is— very strange, just very, very…. I need you to get down here and tell me you're seeing what I'm seeing!"

Ah, now it all makes sense! She didn't die before becoming a mother. She couldn't have! "On my way," said Jen. She hung up and grabbed her coat. She stopped and gave Dugg a scratch behind his ears.

"See you later, boy," she said. "I'm going to see Grandma."

www.ingramcontent.com/pod-product-compliance
Lightning Source LLC
Chambersburg PA
CBHW030751190726

48285CB00003B/808